THE CRUCIBLE

Book 2 of the Siren Song Trilogy

By B.A. Blackwood

www.bablackwood.com

To Ann- my surrogate mom

Love,

ISBN – 978-0-9904367-1-3
Flights of Fancy Publishing House, LLC
Dallas, TX

Library of Congress Control Number: 2018913950

CHAPTER ONE

Crucible: A severe trial or test

I clapped my hand over my nose the second I inhaled the odd, rusty smell. I concentrated on not throwing up, while another part of my brain wondered how bad the stench would be if the room weren't cold enough to drive a bear into hibernation. Was that why they kept this cell only marginally warmer than an igloo? After all, cold air doesn't carry odor very well.

My brain files away useless factoids without even trying, kind of like when a sports nut can reel off their baseball idol's batting average without checking the program. I know that smelling anything in chilly air is problematic because the olfactory receptors in our noses burrow in more deeply to protect themselves. When you couple that with the fact that the speed of an odor molecule moving in hot versus cold air drops from a sprint to a crawl, meaning that fewer molecules ever make it to our buried odor receptors to be recognized, I shouldn't be smelling much of anything.

So why was I gagging? And no, it's not like I'm an expert on the olfactory stages of decay. But some primordial part of my brain, the same part that had me running from spiders as a kid before I even knew what they were, told me what the cloying smell meant.

Someone – or something – had died in this room.

I paced from corner to corner, looking for an escape. I stared at the walls, which hiccupped uneven bubbles as though the sheetrock guy charged with smoothing them had partied a bit too much the night before. I poked one of the blobs with my finger and the whole wall jiggled like an underfilled waterbed. I pushed harder, and tiny waves rippled all the way to the corners of the room.

Maybe the walls were thin enough to break through. I pounded on them with my fists with such force that primeval sounds I hardly recognized as mine escaped from my mouth, sounding eerily like Maria Sharapova's guttural shrieks on the tennis court.

By the way, did you know she's been recorded at a decibel level of 101.2? That's two decibels louder than the sound of a chain saw.

Anyway, I digress.

I gave it all I had, but it was like fighting a giant super-puffed marshmallow. No matter how hard or how many times I hit the same spot, the small indentations I made filled back in before I could even land the next blow.

Arms aching, I sank to the floor. Tears rolled down my cheeks and I didn't bother to wipe them off.

Minutes passed. Tears dripped. Nothing changed.

I swiped at my face. What a wimp. I forced myself to stand up, pulled my jacket down in back where it had ridden up, and straightened my shoulders.

Okay. So, WWED?

I scanned the room, trying to think like Ethan Hunt in the *Mission Impossible* series. No windows, no hidden trap door, no dropped ceiling panel to lift and crawl through, no electronics to short circuit, no object to hone into a knife to kill the guards when they came to get me - not that knives work on them anyway.

Something caught my eye on the far wall. Scratches.

I scurried over and knelt in front of them, peering at the lines. Someone had pressed a makeshift pen deep into the cushiony wall, cutting permanent indentations into it. I squinted at the characters, reading and re-reading them.

I rubbed my eyes and looked again. Nope, I'd seen it right the first time.

If you were being held prisoner by the Enemy with nothing left to hope for except a quick and painless death, would you be working math problems?

CHAPTER TWO

Couthy:
Warm and cozy

Earlier That Day

The air buzzed with secrets. Cyrus and Daniel had been missing in action for days and Barnaby's face wore a look so smug that he might as well have sung "naaa-na-na-naaa-na". Michael just grinned when I begged him to tell me what was going on.

I hate secrets, which is why I'd told Michael when I crawled out of his bed this morning that I had promised to help Barnaby first thing with studying for his Head Doorkeeper exam.

And, not that it's any of your business, but Michael was working late and I fell asleep studying in his room while I waited for him. I'd woken up fully clothed lying on top of the bedcovers to find him dressed and poring over papers on his desk.

"Am I going to see you later today?" I tried not to sound needy.

"I don't know, babe," he said, not lifting his eyes from his work. "I'm slammed."

My face fell. I don't know why I'd bothered to fib about helping Barnaby since Michael was so distracted he probably wouldn't have noticed if I'd left without saying a word.

I've seen the movies where they shoot couples falling in love in honey toned slo-mo. Long meaningful glances, moonlit strolls, whispering secrets to each other, texting constantly when they have to be apart, curling up on the couch together with the t.v. on but being too engrossed in each other to watch it, all set to a romantic musical soundtrack.

That's not us.

Michael has thrown himself into governing, trying to unscramble the damage done by Achimalech. I've been spending all my time either going to class, studying or meeting with the scientists who are trying to figure out how to separate the Piece of Home from me. More on that later.

There's no time to do the things you'd expect of a couple in the throes of true love. It wasn't how I'd pictured the thrill of finding my soulmate.

"Okay." What else was there to say? I'm not going to beg him to spend time with me. I thought you had to be married for at least five years before that happened.

I hustled to the bathroom and examined my face in the mirror. It could be worse. I gave it a once over with a washcloth, swiped some mascara on my eyelashes, and fluffed my hair. Luckily a sweater and jeans don't wrinkle when you sleep in them. Good enough.

I walked over to Michael and kissed his cheek. "I'll be back in a little while".

"Uh huh," he said, the worry wrinkle between his brows not easing a millimeter.

I left, smiling at the ever-present guards outside his room, trying to quell the growing dread that he just wasn't that into me, or at least not as into me as I was into him. It's not like he's a normal boyfriend, so why should I expect him to act like one?

He's got serious responsibilities as the new leader of the Descendants, made more difficult by the fact he doesn't know who might have been Achimalech's collaborators. As wily and charming a character as Achimalech had been, it would be naive to assume that he hadn't recruited anyone else to the dark side. For the moment, Michael only trusts Barnaby, Daniel and Cyrus.

I speed walked through the mountain halls, parking myself around the corner from the Great Kitchen. At precisely 7:58 a.m., Lorinda emerged, balancing a tray with a tall mug and a plate of pastries. Although her head is almost as wide as the tray and her eyes are on the buggy side, she's still cute, kind of like E.T.

Even though I couldn't see exactly what was on the tray, I knew what she carried - a cup of coffee with four sugars and one cream and two chocolate chip scones fresh from the oven with extra sugar crusted on top. Daniel is a creature of habit with a voracious sweet tooth, and Lorinda delivers the same breakfast to him every morning at 8:00 a.m. Wherever Daniel was, Lorinda would find him, and odds were that Cyrus would be with him.

She padded down the glowing corridor towards the east wing. I know it's the east wing only because I've been told so, not because I have any idea which way "east" is. I have directional dyslexia and can't find my own dorm without GPS. Okay, that's exaggerating a bit, but not as much as I'd like. Picture a bat – make it one of those cute, big-eyed cartoon bats, not the scary rabid looking ones – who's born with no sonar, and that pretty much sums up my navigational skills.

I followed at a distance and saw Lorinda come to a stop before a silver door and knock. A few seconds later, the door opened a crack and she disappeared inside. I scurried past and hid behind a curve in the hallway. Lorinda emerged a moment later and headed back toward the Great Kitchen. Once I was sure she was gone, I tiptoed to the door.

Voices I recognized as belonging to Cyrus and Daniel rumbled on the other side of the door. Yes!

I looked both ways. The coast was clear. I leaned forward and pressed my ear against the door.

"...spoiling her." I recognized Daniel's voice.

"Maybe she could...little spoiling," Cyrus' familiar deep voice said.

I pressed my ear harder to the door. I wish I had a water glass to press against the door but, then again, do those things actually work?

"But if you give her everything, she will think money...on trees. Her ambition will be stunted, and she will ... expecting everything to be given to her. Then one day she will wake up ...with no money and no prospects. We might not be there to help her out, and then what? She will spend ...life living on the edge, just barely eking out a living." Lips smacked. "My, this scone...heavenly."

"Come now. Do you really think so?" Cyrus sounded exasperated. Thank goodness his voice carried clearly. "Why can you not just enjoy her, and enjoy giving to her?"

"Why do you insist on making ... the bad guy? I know you want to be – what does Barnaby call it? Oh yes, you want to be ... Disney Dad, but that is not...Raising a child...responsibility." There was a pause, and then Daniel's voice continued, sounding muffled. "You have to ... affect her future."

"You say that every time. Anyway, we are not raising her. We are care-taking. And we are not talking about giving her a diamond necklace or something frivolous like that. It is a computer. I do not think that is over the top. As I understand it, a computer is now a necessity for children."

"It is not."

"Look around. Every child has some sort of computer from at least the age of five on up. And if we do not have a computer with internet access available to her, she will not spend as much time here."

My heart swelled. They wanted me around. They were trying to find ways to get me to spend more time with them, like the parents who buy all the cool gaming equipment and have a pool in the backyard so that their kid will stay home and invite friends to their place rather than going somewhere else.

"Well, I ... just fine without one." Daniel sounded snippy.

"Yes, and you have a goblin attending to your every need. I might take you a little more seriously if you hadn't smeared chocolate on your shirt, which Lorinda will clean for you. You are spoiled on a daily basis."

"Humph." After a long pause, Daniel said, "Okay. But talk to me...before you buy... Do not even ... a car."

I hugged the door, trying to make out Daniel's words.

"Well..."

"Cyrus." Daniel's voice was sharp. "...not need a car."

"She cannot keep borrowing Samantha's car. And the safety ratings on a Volvo are exceptional."

"She can... and transport her everywhere else."

"You know she hates transporting. And the Volvo has those excellent headlights which are essential for coming up winding mountain roads."

With a click the door opened and I fell into the room. The thing-a-ma-jig that kept the door closed hadn't been fully engaged. I tried to keep my balance but ended up sprawling on the floor, elbows first.

Crap.

I squinched my eyes shut, like if I didn't see Daniel and Cyrus, they wouldn't be able to see me.

"Ariel?" Daniel's voice echoed above my head. "Are you okay?"

I kept my eyes shut a second longer and then forced them open. I scrambled to my feet, trying to ignore my throbbing elbows.

"Sorry." My face burned. "But..." I stopped. My mind raced,

trying to come up with some compelling reason to have been pressed against the door. Nothing popped to mind.

"I really have no excuse." I cleared my throat. "I just wanted to know what was going on."

"I knew she would suspect something." Cyrus shook his head at Daniel. "You are terrible at keeping secrets."

"I did not say a word," Daniel said.

Cyrus snorted. "You have been walking around looking like you are about to burst. You perpetually have that supercilious 'I know something you don't' look on your face."

"This isn't my fault." Daniel crossed his arms. "The whole thing would have been done long ago if you did not take so long to make decisions about everything. I swear, you spent a week vacillating between silver and light grey, as though there is some big difference." He sniffed.

"That just shows how color challenged you are. Anyone with taste knows there is a huge difference."

I looked around the room while Daniel and Cyrus carped at each other. My mouth fell open.

Silvery sheer curtains pulled back halfway separated a living area from a bedroom. Behind the glistening curtains, a silver puffy duvet covered a queen-sized bed flanked by rosewood nightstands. Glass-stemmed lamps with silver lampshades rested on each stand, emitting a welcoming glow.

"Wow," I said, stepping further into the room.

On the other side of the curtain, a glass desk settled into a corner with built-in bookshelves on each side. A laptop computer rested atop the desk, and the shelves were filled with books. In the middle of the room sat a curved silver sofa with a cashmere throw draped across its back. A television fit seamlessly into the wall opposite the sofa, and its remote sat on a rosewood side table.

Daniel and Cyrus had stopped fighting, watching me as I took in the room.

"Say something," Cyrus said. His bald head glowed bright red, making him look a bit like a human upended match.

"Is it all right?" Daniel said. "We thought you should have your own place here for when you visit, but we did not know what color to go with or style of furniture, so if it is not to your taste, we can always change it." He twisted the ring on his index finger. "And we have not tried the computer yet. We think we have it hooked up to... to...whatever you hook it up to, but Barnaby was going to check that later today. And..."

"Stop," I said. Tears brimmed in my eyes, and it took me a moment to trust my voice. "This is the most beautiful room I've ever seen. I love it. I can't believe..." I rushed over to Daniel and hugged him tight. I turned to Cyrus and he took a step back, arms raising to ward me off. He's never been big on physical contact. I stopped, and said, "You guys are incredible. Thank you. Thank you so much."

Cyrus beamed.

"Let me show you around," Daniel said.

For the next fifteen minutes, they took me through the whole place, explaining in detail why they'd chosen this or that design, fabric and color. Off the bedroom was a sleek bathroom with a walk-in shower. Hidden cabinets in the walls of the main room revealed a clothes closet and drawers of different sizes.

But the thing that brought tears to my eyes was the framed picture on one of the night stands. I picked it up, tracing the image with my finger. It showed me, my parents, and my twin brothers flung over the bottom of a canoe as though the water had decided it wanted nothing to do with us and had belched us out. Everyone was laughing, even Swisbo (She-Who-Shall-Be-Obeyed, aka Mom), and, for once, we looked like a family, and not a family of four with one outsider - me.

"Where did you get this?" I said, picking up the picture.

"We have our ways," Daniel said, grinning.

I remembered that moment. We'd gone on a family vacation to

Key Largo. My dad had insisted that we could all fit into one canoe to paddle around the mangroves. What he hadn't counted on were my twin brothers, hyped up about being in the ocean for the first time and determined to see who could balance on the side of the canoe. Before we could stop them, the boat had flipped over, and the sight of my always perfectly made up mother with her water-slicked hair and a mangrove leaf stuck to her neck had sent my brothers into laughter so infectious that even Swisbo had lost it and giggled right along with them.

"We wanted you to feel at home here," Cyrus said.

A lump grew in my throat. I'd spent my life wanting to fit into my family, like the nerdy loner in the lunchroom who stares longingly at the next table over where the cool kids swap stories and giggle at each others' jokes.

Even though my dad tries to bridge the gap between me and the rest of the family, I can't help but feel like a bird beating against a glass window, seeing what it wants but unable to break through.

I looked around the room and at Cyrus and Daniel's smiling faces. This felt real. This felt like family. This felt like home.

I'd finally made it through the glass.

"I hate to break up this touching moment, but don't you have to go to class?" The snide voice wiped away all the warm feelings I'd had as quickly as a rat clears a restaurant.

I turned to face my nemesis.

CHAPTER THREE

BILBOES:
AN IRON BAR WITH SLIDING SHACKLES USED TO FASTEN PRISONERS' ANKLES

Sixteen Years Ago: Murder Trial, Day One

he accused walked to the defense table with shuffling steps, as though the titanium shackles in which he'd arrived at the domed Hall of Justice still bound his feet. His knees buckled when he reached the straight-backed wooden chair at the defense table and he landed hard. When he raised his head to look at the jury, though, his face was composed, unlike that of the man sitting to his right, whose expression bounced between fear and anger.

Not a good look for a lawyer defending someone on a murder charge.

The prosecutor rose and strode toward the jury panel, stopping four feet away, just close enough to seem like he wanted to speak to them personally but not so close as to invade their space. Every lawyer has a jury dance, and if it were plotted out it would look like a boxy waltz that doesn't use much of the floor - one step forward, one step sideways, one step backward, one step sideways. The prosecutor knew more about winning over a jury than Albert Einstein knew about the theory of relativity. He'd mastered the jury dance so well that he could get away with broadening the box by a step or two. The very fact that he'd been tapped to try the case by the Head Prosecutor showed how much the Descendants' Council wanted to put the Defendant away.

"Most of you know this man," he said in a conversational yet somber tone, turning and pointing to the Defendant. "I wouldn't be surprised if all of you don't know at least one person he has helped. Up until now, he's had a crystal clean reputation, and rightfully so. His wise counsel and hard work have helped our community time and time again. He's not the kind of gentleman you'd expect to be sitting in a courtroom charged with murder."

"No," the prosecutor continued, shaking his head, "I'm not going to try to persuade you that he's just been hiding an evil nature behind some kind of benign mask. I couldn't do that even if I were foolish enough to try."

"But I don't need to," he said, taking one step towards the jury. "Murder isn't always committed by evil people. In fact, most of the time it's committed in the heat of the moment by a normal person who is threatened with the loss of something precious to them. Something like love or power or reputation." He drew out the last few words and looked at each of the jurors in turn with his brown, serious eyes.

"The evidence will show you that, in fact, Rachel Scarborough was killed precisely because of those three things – the Defendant's loss of her love and the irreparable damage the Defendant feared would come to his power and reputation."

"You see, the Defendant fell hard for Rachel. I know," he said, raising his hand as though to stop a protest, "it seems hard to believe that a man the Defendant's age, with his piercing intelligence, would fall in love with such a young and – let's be frank – foolish woman. But the Defendant's hallowed perch in our society and his loneliness made him very susceptible to someone like Rachel. She woke in him that precious thing called hope, with disastrous consequences."

He walked over to a video screen facing the jury panel and passed his hand in front of it. A woman appeared on the screen, tucking a daisy behind the ear of a delighted little girl, looking like a young, and very beautiful, Mother Teresa.

"Most of you knew Rachel, and, as you also know, her reputation was a bit spotty," the prosecutor continued, his face taking on a regretful expression. "Like many young people, she hadn't yet found her way."

"Yes," he said, walking back to the jury rail, "she was known as being flighty, somewhat lazy, and unreliable except when it came to children. She loved children, spent time volunteering in the nursery, and undoubtedly would have grown into a credit to our community. But she had no family, no brothers or sisters, to guide her. Her family had all been taken in the Great Conflagration, so she was totally on her own."

The faces of four of the jurors softened, while others nodded their heads. They all remembered the patriots who had died in the Great Conflagration, a bitter war in which the Enemy had tried to wipe out the Descendants once and for all. Many had died in the seven bloody days that the battle had raged. The Descendants had beaten the Enemy back, but at great cost.

"Rachel grew up shuttled from distant relative to distant relative, none of whom took any great interest in her." The prosecutor hesitated for a moment. "Just imagine what that kind of upbringing – treated as nobody special, with no mother or father who thinks you hung the moon - would do to someone who turns from the proverbial ugly duckling into a swan." He took a step forward, standing within a foot of the jury box.

"For the first time in her life, people noticed her, men wanted to be around her, she was treated as exceptional - all because of her looks. The power at her fingertips was intoxicating, and, like a child who first experiences the wonders of the taste of chocolate, she got carried away." The prosecutor rested a hand on the jury rail.

"Rachel used her charms indiscriminately, experimenting with them, not appreciating the power those charms had or the danger they could cause." His speech quickened. "She broke engagement after engagement, used her charms to snare whoever she took a passing fancy to, discarded one conquest for another." He shook his head. "If she'd had a mother, or a close female relative, or even a father, they could have helped guide her through the discovery of her newfound allure. But she did not."

"And, frankly, our community let her down." The prosecutor's normally strident tone softened. He took a step back. "Sure, we gave her food, shelter, education – the basics. But we didn't take her in like a daughter or a sister. We didn't fill the void that her parents left."

"So can we really blame her for her thoughtless flirting? She wasn't some kind of a Jezebel." He held his hands out as though in supplication. "She was just a young, immature woman, who hadn't yet mastered the nuances and yes, the dangers, of her beauty." The prosecutor dropped his hands and straightened, taking a sideways step.

"This isn't a tale of depravity run amok between a blacker-than-coal man and a whiter-than-snow woman." His voice had taken on the rhythmic cadence of a seasoned storyteller. "Those only exist in fairy tales. It's far simpler. It's a story about a beautiful woman wielding her newfound powers of seduction on a lonely man past his prime, widowed for years, hungry for the attention and intimacy that only a woman could bring."

"What was just a fling for her was serious business to him. Imagine his surprise, and then his delight, to discover that Rachel wanted to spend time with him." The prosecutor gestured to the image of Rachel on the screen, shaking his head as though in wonder. "He'd probably never figured in his wildest dreams that such a young, lovely woman would find him attractive."

"And then imagine his anger, his embarrassment, his humiliation, his awful shame when he found he'd meant nothing to her, that she'd moved on to someone else. All that hope torn from him. All those dreams he'd had for a new life – gone."

"But that wasn't the real kicker." The prosecutor paused and took a step forward, lowering his voice conspiratorially, as though letting them in on a secret.

"More than that, a man known for his intelligence and reason, a pillar of the community, one to whom others turned for advice," he said, turning to look at the Defendant for a beat. "This man – a man who took enormous pride in his solid reputation and the power he wielded in community matters - had been made to look like a common fool."

"Unsurprisingly, the Defendant denies that he had anything to do with Rachel's death." The prosecutor straightened and his voice changed from that of a storyteller to the confident, crisp diction of a man who'd never lost a case. "But the evidence against him is rock solid."

"First," he said, holding up one finger, "we have a witness who saw Rachel on January 14 of this year in the middle of a shouting confrontation with the Defendant. After that violent argument, Rachel was never seen again."

"Second," the prosecutor said, holding up another finger, "Rachel's blood was found in the Defendant's car. The Defendant says that they were never together anywhere except in his office and his office parking lot, but blood evidence doesn't lie."

"Third," he said as another finger popped up on his hand,

"Rachel's purse with her i.d. and wallet were found in the Defendant's home."

"Fourth, fragments of clothing identified as hers were found both in the field where she was murdered and partially burned in his fireplace." The prosecutor waved four fingers in front of the jury before dropping his hand to his side. He took a step back toward the jury box.

"You don't have to find that the Defendant was a homicidal maniac to convict him. He wasn't. That's why we're not asking you to impose the death penalty. No, this was a crime of passion committed by a lonely, heartbroken, humiliated old man in the heat of the moment."

The defense lawyer tried to keep a stoic expression, but inside his heart sank. Both the Defendant's and Rachel's characters had been effectively neutralized. He'd hoped that the Prosecutor would try to paint the Defendant as a bad seed who'd been lurking behind a façade of good works and Rachel as a virginal innocent. He'd planned to knock those images down, and in the process cast doubt on the entire case.

But the prosecutor had sidestepped that pitfall. The defense lawyer – the one the Defendant had insisted take the case, and, truth be known, the only lawyer who would agree to take the case – choked down the bile burning in his throat.

Lucian Castlewhite's first murder trial was turning into the nightmare he'd always known it would be.

CHAPTER FOUR

CONTRIVANCE: A PLAN OR SCHEME

Remember the time Lex Luther invented a hybrid polymer-based flight suit to protect Superman from Kryptonite? Or when the Great Orc Army stormed Smaug the Terrible's lair and saved Bilbo Baggins from being burned alive? Or that wild gunfight at Gotham City Hall when the Joker dove through the air and took a bullet for Batman?

Yeah. I don't either.

I knew when Michael stuck me with Rosamund as my bodyguard that the situation might be problematic. Sure, she's got Jackie Chan moves and can pin a greased-up Sumo wrestler to the floor in two seconds flat. But she's not terribly motivated to protect me.

Actually, she hates my guts – something about stealing her fiancée, which, for the record I didn't do. They were broken up way before I came on the scene.

Really.

I'd come this close to getting knee callouses begging Michael to assign someone else as my protector, but he'd insisted that Rosamund would do her job regardless of her personal feelings, not because of some ingrained professional code, but because if the Enemy got me, they'd get the Piece of Home and then we'd all be doomed. He'd also thrown in that my personal bodyguard had to be a woman so that she could pose as my roommate, and Rosamund was the absolute best they had.

It had all sounded so logical at the time. And, when Michael fixed me with TBD - The Blue Daze, smoldering blue orbs heating up under charcoal eyelashes - I couldn't dredge up my phone number, much less the reasons why a pampered toy poodle would be a better bodyguard for me than Rosamund.

Besides, the only thing I know about self-defense came from a $25 course taught by a sweaty ex-cop in a strip shopping center. Swisbo had forced me to go, her adamant insistence the only sign that she might be uneasy about her daughter going over a thousand miles away from home to college.

I learned two things in the class. First, no matter how perfectly I executed the *Deashi Harai*, or "sweep and drop the dirt bag" maneuver, sheer physics dictated that the only dirt bag my height-challenged self could force to the ground would be a guy standing no taller than five feet six inches coming off a three-week cleansing fast.

Second, the Don't-Be-An-Idiot defense – travel in pairs, don't go out late at night, keep an eagle eye out while walking instead of texting, always tell someone where you're going – doesn't help me at all. I could hole up in my room and never come out except in broad daylight to attend Sunday School escorted by a flock of Bible-carrying deacons and it wouldn't keep me safe. The Enemy is coming after me, and no amount of "safety first" dogma will change that.

In other words, me providing for my own protection is out of the question.

Ergo, Rosamund.

"Let's go Weenie".

"I asked you not to call me that." I glared at her.

She gave me a beatific smile. She claimed the nickname was a shortened version of "Teeny-Weeny", but I knew better. No one wants to be called Weeny and she knows it.

"Say goodbye to Daniel and Cyrus," she said, and before I could open my mouth, she'd grabbed me and several excruciating seconds later we were standing in my dorm room. I know Rosamund can transport more quickly. I think she just drags it out to torment me.

I huffed into the bathroom, took a quick shower and came back out dressed and ready to go ten minutes later. Glaring at Rosamund, I grabbed my books and stuffed them haphazardly into my backpack. Rosamund had managed to suck all the warmth of Daniel and Cyrus' amazing gift out of me, leaving me in a grinchy mood. Not helping matters was the fact that my first class was Intro to Philosophy, a beating of a class which had shot to the top of my least favorite list after only one week and had remained there, even edging out Organic Chemistry.

I stomped out of the room and set off across campus, ducking my head against the cold. Snowflakes stung my face, the wind turning them into icy projectiles. In my rush to get away from Rosamund, I'd forgotten my woolen cap. I shivered, picking up the pace. Hadn't I read that more heat escapes through your head than any other part of your body? By the time I made it to the building where my class was, I'd speeded up to a trot. As I flew through the door, my phone dinged with a text message from my lawyer.

Yes, I'm seventeen years old and I have a lawyer – Lucian Castlewhite. And no, I'm not running from the law or the heiress to some huge fortune that requires legions of professionals.

I wish.

I'm an ordinary girl with only two out of the ordinary features. I'm petite, parent-speak for this-close-to-being-a-midget short, and I'm obsessed with words to the point that I won't take an overnight trip without my five word-a-day calendars. Some might say my word passion is a tad monomaniacal (an inordinate or obsessive interest in a subject) but I prefer to think of it as a harmless quirk. I mean, when have you ever seen a public service announcement warning about the dangers of knowing too many words?

It's not that I don't like Lucian. In fact, he's turned out to be one of my favorite people, a grandfatherly type with a cut-throat shark streak which pops out just at the right time.

But Lucian never texts. I didn't even know he had a cell phone. In fact, I'm positive he and his secretary, Mrs. Spicklemeyer, still use the 1950's era black rotary dial phones like you see in the noir movies on the granny channel, like *Dial M for Murder* or *Sorry Wrong Number*.

So the minute I made out who the text was from my stomach did a little flip. For Lucian to find a phone and learn how to text meant something big was up.

I squinted at the message. "Derr Arrel: Hope al iss gll with yu and tht your studcies are nt tooo taaxin. A mttter of sme urrgexcy has ariisenm and I ndd to sppeke to you. Pleeeese call me. Yors Trullly, Luciian Castlhjhite"

I chuckled, imagining Lucian's big thumbs trying to find the right letters on a tiny phone and then squinting through his glasses at the minute characters on the screen. He's as myopic as Mr. Magoo, so I guessed he'd just had to hope for the best while he typed.

I walked to my desk and sat down, trying to make sense of the message. I'd call him when I got out of class. It couldn't be that big a deal if he'd sent a text instead of coming to see me in person, his usual mode of communication. And he hadn't said call immediately, so I figured it could wait. I started to text back but, at that moment, the room fell silent.

I looked up to see Professor Muldrow staring pointedly at my phone. He'd made it very clear on the first day of class that if he caught anyone using a phone in class he'd throw it away. I glanced up at the wall clock and saw the second hand sweeping up toward the top of the hour. I shut the phone off, unzipped my backpack and threw it in with two seconds to spare before the official start of class.

Professor Muldrow shook his head and stalked to the front of the room just as Samantha, my suitemate and best friend, ran into class, love beads a la Partridge Family clacking around her neck.

Here's the difference between me and Samantha. She's got one of those open faces that you just can't help liking, and her eyes regard everyone - even the snootiest sorority girl or the scariest looking tattooed biker - with a look that says, "I think you're wonderful and I just know we're going to be friends." A tinge of melancholy behind her eyes hints that her openness is purposeful and not simply innocence, which makes her all the more appealing.

If I'd come in a couple of seconds late, Professor Muldrow would probably have kicked me out of class. Being tardy was right up there with using a cell phone on his pet peeve list, but you'd never know it by the faint smile on his face as Samantha beamed at him and slid into the seat next to mine at the back of the classroom.

As I listened to Professor Muldrow drone on about Marcus Aurelius, a cold sweat broke out on my forehead. This had been happening more and more lately. I'd counted on the class to calm me down, since normally Professor Muldrow's lectures act on me like a double dose of Ambien, but instead my pulse kept clipping along at Indy 500 speeds.

I shrank down in my seat, taking deep cleansing breaths like I'd seen on Samantha's yoga dvd. The instructors always look so peaceful and in control as they contort into torture-chamber shapes that should send any ordinary person straight to a chiropractor. Samantha assured me it was all in the breathing.

Uh huh.

I guess feeling like a netful of butterflies had been released in my stomach was pretty normal considering all I had going on. Maybe my life would seem more manageable if I just broke everything down into simple tasks. Hadn't some wise Chinese guy said that a journey of a thousand miles begins with a single step?

I flipped through the pages of my notepad until I came to a clean one. The sheet was one of those with ruler-straight horizontal blue lines intersected on the left by one red vertical one, the kind of orderly expanse that begs for clinical detail and objective thinking. Just looking at it made me feel more in control.

I reached under my desk and dug out the mechanical pencil with the really fine tip from my backpack that I use in calculus class to squeeze ten-digit numbers into tiny spaces and began to write with the care of a professional calligrapher, trying to match the crisp clarity of the neatly lined page.

TO DO

1. Figure out how to keep the Piece of Home out of the Enemy's hands forever.
2. Figure out how to keep the Enemy from killing/hurting/maiming me while accomplishing #1 above.
3. Work through relationship issues with Michael.
4. Find out the identity of my father and more facts about my mother in between doing items ##1 through 3 above.

There. My first step. I stared at the list, waiting to feel the Zen of someone with a game plan.

Nada. If anything, my pulse notched up a tick.

I wanted to bang my head on the desk. It's not that I asked to be stuck with the Piece of Home. I'd love to unload the thing if I could just figure out how to do it. But – and I say this with all seriousness and not one touch of freshman diva drama – the fate of the entire world depends on what happens to the Piece of Home.

I stared back down at the list. Maybe I was trying to tackle someone else's thousand-mile journey. After all, the Piece of Home isn't really my responsibility. The only reason I've still got it is that for some weird reason I'm the only one who can hold the thing. Literally.

The Piece of Home burns the hands off of anyone who tries to take it from me. I'm just holding onto it until the Exiles and Descendants, aka The Good Guys, decide what to do with it, kind of like babysitting a kid whose parents are away on a date night. And just like parents who wouldn't want harm to come to the person keeping their baby safe, the Good Guys have every reason to want me alive and kicking.

The truth is I'm probably safer than anyone on the Montana State campus. After all, I've got a phalanx of guards posted all over campus to intercept the bad guys and protect me, or at least that's what they tell me. I can't actually see them.

I tried not to think about the recurring dream I have in which a naked figure with man boobs resting atop a watermelon stomach struts down the street sporting his imaginary expensive threads while the shocked onlookers whisper, "but the Emperor has no new clothes" and cover their children's eyes.

Nope, you don't have to be Freud to get that one. But, it had been almost a month since I'd found the Piece of Home and I hadn't had any close shaves, so I'm pretty sure the guards are out there watching over me.

The more I thought about it the better I felt. If anybody is up for the job of figuring out what to do with the Piece of Home and keeping me safe, it's The Good Guys. After all, they're the Fallen Angels and their offspring who chose to go straight, unlike the Enemy, who stuck with Satan. Any group brave and smart enough to betray the most evil being in the universe and live to tell about it has to be pretty tough. They should be able to pull this off.

I blew out the breath I hadn't even known I'd been holding. I wrote "NMP" – not my problem – by items one and two.

As for working through relationship issues with Michael, none of them are deal breakers. They're little things, like how do we carve out time to spend together when he has a pretty demanding day job and I'm trying to master Calculus and Biology, and what kind of a life span does he have since he's half Fallen Angel and half human and will that have any effect on us, and would he consider driving a car to take me places so that I don't have to let him transport me Star Trek style all the time (oh how I've come to loathe that word "transport"), and why do I still get a cramp in my stomach when I see he and his ex-fiancee interact with each other even though he swears that he never really loved her, and why won't he carry his cell phone at all times so that people can reach him, for cripes sake.

See? They're minor problems, really. I'm secretly thrilled down to my toenails to have an actual relationship, even if we do have a few kinks to work out. I've used the word "boyfriend" about a million times in the last month, feeling the same glow of wellbeing, of belonging, of "yes someone incredible actually wants to be with me" pride every single time it rolls off my tongue.

I never dreamed I'd fall in love so fast and with someone as mind-blowingly wonderful as Michael. And I'm 99% sure that he loves me. So that's all that really matters, right - that we love each other? After all, every gripping love story I've read has "love conquers all" as its underlying theme, and they all live happily ever after against tremendous odds, except for *Romeo and Juliet*, but come on, the whole death thing could have been avoided with better communication skills. Oh, and, of course, *Gone With The Wind*, but we all know in our heart of hearts there's no way Scarlett won't get Rhett back.

I mean, if a supernatural being descended from angels falling in love with a height-challenged nothing-special human from Dallas, Texas isn't an against all odds love story I don't know what is. By the reckoning of all the great love stories, rom/com movies, and love ballads dating back to Shakespeare's time, Michael and I should be able to overcome anything.

I wrote "NARP" - not a real problem – by item number three.

That only left one task, number four, getting the low-down on my real parents. That shouldn't be too hard since my bio-mom left a detailed log. It's mostly about archaeology stuff, but it should give me a better sense of her, and surely she'd have recorded at least a tiny clue as to who my real father is.

If something as big as getting pregnant happened to you, wouldn't you be bursting to say something about it? Like, "Can't climb the south rim of the Grand Canyon for a few months because I'm pregnant by the most fabulous man in the world! Yay!!!!!!!!"

I tried not to think about all the other possible entries. Ones like "can't believe I slept with that hairy Neanderthal and now look at the mess I'm in," or, even worse, "stuck in the office trying not to slit my wrists because just discovered I'm pregnant with unknown rapist's child." I clamped down on those thoughts and banished them before they could breed even nastier ideas and cause me nightmares.

I'm pretty good at that sort of thing. What some people call naivete I call positive thinking.

My pulse had slowed down to near normal levels. I really only had one thing to do on my list – find out about my real parents – and that's a matter of curiosity, not life or death. I have a perfectly good set of parents, even if we don't share DNA. The displaced feeling I sometimes get around my adoptive family is nothing compared to the life and death issues involved in the Piece of Home, which I'd just established were NMP.

So, the whole bio-family thing was not that big of a deal. It was a fun problem really, just something to look into when I had the time, like an enjoyable research project. I wrote "FP" – fun problem - by item number 4.

Then I went back and added smiley faces, just to underline the point that these were either all handled or not really that big of a deal.

I sat back in my chair and looked at my revised list.

1. *Figure out how to keep the Piece of Home out of the Enemy's hands forever.* **NMP** 😐
2. *Figure out how to keep the Enemy from killing/hurting/maiming me while accomplishing #1 above.* **NMP** 😐
3. *Work through relationship issues with Michael.* **NARP** 😐
4. *Find out the identity of my father and more facts about my mother in between doing items ##1 through 3 above.* **FP** 😐

Everything was going to be okay after all. My thousand-mile journey had turned into a barely-breaking-a-sweat ten mile stroll.

Uh huh. Sometimes I take the whole Polyanna thing a bit too far.

CHAPTER FIVE

ABSTRUSE:
HARD TO UNDERSTAND

pen jabbed me in the ribs and I turned around to see Samantha, eyes wide, mouthing something.

"What?" I whispered.

"Ariel?"

Whoops. Professor Muldrow stood two feet away, looking at me with a frown.

"Liebniz's theory. Did you read the material?"

I smoothed my face into what I hoped looked like knowledgeable lines.

"Yes. Gottfried Wilhelm Liebniz."

Professor Muldrow nodded. Now, if I just had a clue as to what the question was.

"His Theory of Optimism. Could you explain it to the class?"

For about the millionth time I regretted choosing Philosophy as an elective. I thought it would be a nice break from chemistry, calculus, and biology. In other words, an easy A.

Wrong.

Trying to wrap my mind around centuries old philosophers' musings just gave me a raging headache and zero enlightenment. I racked my brain for Liebniz's theory.

The muscles in my neck loosened. I had this one.

"His theory was that the world we live in is the best possible world that God could have created."

There. Crisis averted. I looked back down at my pad and started writing as though taking studious notes.

"And how did he reach that conclusion?"

No one answered, and I looked up to see Professor Muldrow still staring at me.

Uh huh. So this was his payback for the near miss with the phone.

It wasn't as though I hadn't read the material. I'm obsessive that way. I feel compelled to read the assignments, even while being stalked by supernatural beings who want to end the world as we know it.

No, that wasn't the problem. I'd read it. I just didn't have a clue what it meant.

When I said nothing, Professor Muldrow looked around the room. "Anyone?"

No one moved. Apparently I wasn't the only one in the dark. Thank goodness.

He turned to the blackboard and wrote out the entire reasoning in his precise handwriting, using both of the huge blackboards covering the entire front wall of the room. I'm including what he wrote verbatim just so you can see what I'm up against in this class. I've read the thing several times, but my mind always starts skittering sideways somewhere under No. 4.

(1) God is omnipotent *and* omniscient *and* benevolent *and* the free creator of the world. (Definition)

(2) Things could have been otherwise—i.e., there are other possible worlds. (Premise)
(3) Suppose this world is *not* the best of all possible worlds. (i.e., "The world could be better.")
(4) If this world is not the best of all possible worlds, then at least one of the following must be the case:
- God was not powerful enough to bring about a better world; or
- God did not know how this world would develop after his creation of it (i.e. God lacked foreknowledge); or
- God did not wish this world to be the best; or
- God did not create the world; or
- there were no other possible worlds from which God could choose.

(5) But, any one or more of the disjuncts of (4) contradicts (1) or (2).
(6) Therefore, this world is the best of all possible worlds.

See – total Greek. Worse than Organic Chemistry.

"Okay people." Professor Muldrow looked at his watch. "We're out of time. Next week there will be a quiz on what Liebniz meant. You'll need to dig into some of the extra reading on your syllabus."

Groans erupted around the room, which only made Professor Muldrow smile.

What a sadist.

I gathered my books, shaking my head at Samantha who was headed toward Professor Muldrow.

"It won't work," I mouthed to her, knowing she hoped to flatter her way from a "C" to a "B" in the class.

She waggled her fingers at me, grinning and then called, "Hey, don't forget lunch with my parents."

"I'll be there." I waved at her and headed toward the door. The hall swarmed with students eager to escape, most probably heading to Bridger Bowl to get in some skiing before their afternoon classes.

I edged into the crowd, buffeted by elbows and oversized backpacks and allowed the human stream to propel me out the door.

And then I saw him.

Michael stood at the bottom of the stairs looking like a modern day blue-eyed Rhett Butler. I jammed my to-do list into my coat pocket and ran down the steps toward him.

Every time I see Michael I move at lickety-split speed to get to him like you see in those *Sleepless-In-Seattle*-type moments replicated over and over in every romantic movie. You know, the one where Katie or Kristie or Kathy doesn't realize until it's almost too late that she's about to lose the love of her life, and she has to run through buckets of rain in her Jimmy Choo stilettos because her piece of crap car won't start or her Uber app won't work or all cab drivers are on strike to find her soulmate before he marries Betty from accounting or signs up for a three year Army tour in Afghanistan or takes a research job in Antarctica.

Pathetic, I know, but I can't help myself.

I skidded to a stop in front of him and looked up into those light blue eyes, basking in the warm gaze he turned on me.

"I thought you were tied up today," I said, unable to wipe the grin off my face.

"I missed you." Okay, this was more like the romance novels I'd read in secret growing up and stuffed under my mattress away from prying eyes.

"Besides, walking you home from class is one of my favorite parts of the day." He brushed a piece of hair back from my face, ignoring the staring gaggle of girls walking by. "Why is it again that you have to go to class?"

"So I won't be a thirty year old living with my parents slurping down Ramen noodles because I can't find a job."

He snagged my hand in his and we began walking down the sidewalk. Even through my mittens I couldn't help feeling a bit tingly as his fingers squeezed mine.

"Well, you now have a room at the mountain."

I threw a quick glance at him.

"Yes, I heard. I told Daniel and Cyrus they'd better speed it up or you'd figure it out. I just hope you didn't hurt yourself when you fell into the room." He grinned at me. "And I'd throw in the Ramen noodles for free."

I laughed.

"I'm serious," he said. "You could move in to the mountain until we get all this sorted out."

My mind whirled. Moving into my new beautiful room full time, seeing Michael every day, being surrounded by the entire bulwark of the Descendants' defenses, seeing Michael every day, getting to hang out with my best goblin bud Barnaby, seeing Michael every day...

But for some reason, I couldn't form the word "yes". I wanted to try to keep a normal life, relatively speaking, and I wasn't so besotted (16th century word meaning foolishly affectionate, like getting a heart-shaped "Michael and Ariel Forever" tattooed on my shoulder blade) that I wanted to sit around waiting for him to make an appearance in between meetings.

Who knows, maybe I was secretly a little intimidated by Michael's new position. The fact that he's a Descendant is scary enough, but now that he's the Leader of the Descendants for the Northern Hemisphere, he has the equivalent of the CIA, army, navy, and air force multiplied times ten and on steroids at his fingertips. The President of the United States just THINKS he's the most powerful being on the planet. My little dorm room gave me a modicum of normality, and I can pretend that I'm just a typical freshman for almost twenty whole minutes when I'm there.

Michael stopped walking and pulled me close, looking down at me with TBD. My knees shook a little. Then again, maybe that tattoo wouldn't look so bad.

"Just think about it." He kissed me lightly on the lips, and began walking again, tucking my arm in his.

"By the way," he said, "I think we may have the Piece of Home figured out."

"You know how to destroy it?"

He shook his head. "I think we've almost figured out how to contain it so that you can give it to us and the Enemy would have no reason to be interested in you anymore."

"Really?" I said, a grin spreading across my face.

"Really."

Here's the deal. No one else can hold the Piece of Home without getting burned. If I try to lay it on the floor, put it in a box, or detach myself from it in anyway, it boomerangs right back to me as though attached by an invisible bungee cord.

Last time I'd been at the Descendants' headquarters, they'd constructed a steel box they were sure would do the trick. Instead, the Piece of Home burst through it, shredding the steel and scattering tiny shrapnel all over the place. A couple of the techs were still picking the bits out of their skin.

I gave myself a mental pat on the back. I'd been so right about the Piece of Home being not my problem.

I shivered as a wisp of icy wind managed to find the one tiny opening in my jacket. I pulled it more tightly around me, wondering again why the same year I start school at Montana State, they record the earliest and coldest winter on record. Even the snow-laden pine trees seemed over the whole thing, their branches sagging even lower than usual.

"You need a warmer coat," he said.

"This is the industrial version, guaranteed to have more down than an entire flock of geese. And I have a sweater and a turtleneck on under that. It's just too cold here."

He stopped and took his coat off, draping it around me. I secretly love this. He does it all the time. I could have put on a couple more layers, but I love the feel and smell of Michael's coat. He only wears it for show anyway. He doesn't seem to feel the cold.

"Hey," I said. "I'm going to meet Samantha's parents for lunch today. They're up a day early for Parent's Weekend. Do you want to meet afterward?"

"Sorry, I wish I could. I've got a lot to do, and I want to get as much done as I can before your parents get here."

Pleasure tinged with anxiety made my stomach do a flip. Swisbo and Dad are coming today, and Michael seems eager to meet them. I'm dying to introduce them to Michael because how in the world could they not be impressed with him?

On the other hand, where Swisbo is concerned, anything could go wrong. She has no compunction about sharing her true feelings when it involves something non-society related, either through an icy stare, or a slight turn-down of the corners of her mouth, or actually walking away without saying a word.

Dad, on the other hand, is super-cool, partly because he really is, and partly, I suspect, because he's trying to make up for Swisbo's behavior.

I saw with dismay that we'd already reached my dorm. Michael lifted his coat from my shoulders and put it back on.

"So," he said, "I'll meet you at the restaurant at seven?"

I nodded. "Just don't expect too much from my mom."

"I know, I know," he said, holding up his hands. "You've warned me about her at least a hundred times. Whether she loves me or hates me, I'm pretty sure I can handle it."

"Yeah, that's what everyone says until they meet her," I muttered.

"Quit worrying," he said, kissing me lightly. "See you then. And get inside before you freeze to death."

"Do you really have to go? Can't you hang out for just a little while?"

"I wish," he said. "But at least I skipped out long enough to see you. I just wanted to walk you home from class. I miss doing that."

"Me too," I said. "My new bodyguard isn't quite the same. I'm still hoping you'll come up with someone else."

"She's not so bad," Michael said, turning to go. "Give her a little time."

"I've given her a month. Instead of things getting easier, they're actually getting worse," I said.

"I know you haven't seen the good side of her..." Michael said, turning back.

I snorted.

"But she's actually a very sweet girl."

"Did you say sweet?" I said, gaping at him.

"Yes," he said firmly. "You just haven't seen that yet."

"The average life span for a human female is 81.48 years. I don't think I'm going to see it before I die," I said.

He shook his head at me as he started back down the sidewalk.

"Hey," I said, calling after him. "Turn your cell phone on. No one can reach you if it's not on."

"You mean you can't reach me if it's not on," he said, grinning.

"Exactly. So turn it on already," I said, giving him a mock glare.

"I'll do it just for you. I'll even call you later," he said over his shoulder.

I waved at him and then made my way into the dorm. I sighed, thinking of Rosamund. Maybe I was being too hard on her. It couldn't be easy being stuck babysitting me. Maybe I should try to walk a mile in her shoes for a change. It might give me a whole new perspective on her.

But then I opened the door to my room moments later and took in the mess that was my roommate's side of our living space.

Nah. She was a nightmare.

CHAPTER SIX

GUDDLE:
TO FISH WITH ONE'S HANDS BY GROPING UNDER THE STONES OR BANKS OF A STREAM

Sixteen Years Ago: Murder Trial, Evening of the First Day

"Enos, come on in. Tell me you found something," Lucian said to his investigator. "I've got to have more than SODDI. Otherwise, we're dead in the water."

A man strode into the room, walking with an athlete's grace in his ostrich skin cowboy boots. He wore no-name jeans and a cowboy shirt faded and softened from hundreds of washings, but that's where ordinary stopped. Lean muscle covered his body, steely eyes flashed from under hooded lids and his face could have been chiseled from stone. He looked dangerous, like a coiled snake waiting to strike.

Enos sank into the worn leather chair opposite Lucian's desk, pulled a stick of gum from his packet, unwrapped it, and folded it into his mouth.

"I don't have anything that would let us point specifically to someone else," he said between chews, knowing Lucian was talking about the "Some Other Dude Did It" defense.

Lucian's shoulders slumped.

"I've looked over the prosecution's evidence," Enos said. "It's pretty skinny. Can't you get where you need to be just on the absence of any real evidence connecting our guy to Rachel?"

"No," Lucian said. "That only works when I have a category of people to blame. Like a pawnshop owner who might have disgruntled customers who want their stuff back after it's already been sold, or a priest who has heard confessions that you could argue someone would be afraid would be disclosed. Unfortunately, in this case I've only got a silly girl with no criminal connections who no one cared enough about to kill. I'm afraid it's going to be like that notorious Peterson case. I don't want to be haunted by a bird for the rest of my life."

"A bird?" Enos raised one eyebrow. "Do tell."

"You remember that author in North Carolina who was accused of murdering his wife?"

Enos shook his head.

"Michael Peterson found his wife at the bottom of the stairs, covered in blood, and the amount of blood was more than anyone could really explain by a simple fall down the stairs. She had deep gashes on the top of her head which had caused most of the bleeding. The police arrested Peterson and the prosecution claimed that he'd beaten her. He was convicted of murder and sentenced to life without the possibility of parole."

"And we care about this because..." Enos spread his hands.

"The defense did a superb job of poking holes in the prosecution's case, and basically proved that a beating such as the prosecution described would have resulted in a skull fracture or brain swelling, which Mrs. Peterson did not have. They put on experts that made the prosecution's experts look like kindergarteners. But the woman had no enemies, no unsavory life style choices, no skeletons in the closet, nothing about her that would have provoked anyone to kill her. There was nothing missing and no evidence of an intruder. The defense offered no solid alternate theory for how she ended up dead. Their entire defense rested on attacking the forensic evidence – nothing sexy, just taking apart the science. But it didn't work."

"Well, maybe Peterson did it," Enos said.

"I'm pretty sure he didn't." Lucian leaned forward, resting his elbows on his desk. "The problem was the defense had no story to tell. A jury has to be able to see – to feel – what happened. It doesn't matter if you massacre all the prosecution's experts. If you don't give the jury a story to latch onto, it's hard for them not to convict. In Peterson's case, the prosecution had a story. The defense did not. It was game over before they even started."

Enos' brow creased. "Why are you so stuck on the Peterson case? Did you know someone in the case?"

"No. But this case is reminding me of it. Peterson is now out of prison, for reasons that don't matter for our purposes, but the real kicker is that the wife was most likely killed by an owl."

Enos whistled through his teeth.

"I know. It sounds fantastic but it's true. Years after the crime, it came out that owl feathers were found near her body and in her scalp, the wounds were consistent with what would come from a bird's claws, there were microscopic particles in the wounds from tree limbs, and owl attacks had happened in that area before. She was probably attacked by an owl outside, ran inside, fell and hit her head on the bottom of the stairs."

"You've got to be kidding me," Enos said. Now he was the one leaning forward.

"I wish I were," Lucian said, steepling his fingers. "The defense couldn't figure out a good theory for how Mrs. Peterson ended up where she did with all the blood and the wounds on her head, so they had to go with simply attacking the prosecution's experts. It never occurred to anyone that an owl could have done it. I mean, who would ever think of that?" He sighed.

"I can't imagine getting sent to prison for a murder that was committed by an owl," Enos said, shaking his head. "Peterson has to be the unluckiest guy in the world."

"I don't think it's any coincidence that most of my nightmares now have an owl in them somewhere." Lucian massaged his temples as though relieving a headache. "We're missing something. I have to come up with a plausible theory that the jury can see happening. Otherwise it doesn't matter how well I cross-examine their experts. We'll lose."

Both men sat in silence. The lamps in the room fought against the black night waiting just outside the windows. The only sound in the room was the pendulum of an old grandfather clock swinging back and forth in its glass case.

"There might be something," Enos said.

"What is it?" Lucian straightened.

"There are several weekends – and even some weekdays – in the months before her death when no one seems to know where Rachel was."

"Tell me more," Lucian said, hope animating his face.

"That's just it. There is nothing more. I've hit a dead end. Rachel had no real girlfriends that I can find, no confidantes, so there's no one I can ask. She had no family. She didn't have to work weekends at Headquarters, and the time she took off during the week was covered in her vacation time. No one knows where she went, and apparently no one cared enough to ask at the time."

"That sounds she was sneaking off to be with someone inappropriate, like a married man," Lucian said.

"Yep," Enos said, flicking a spot of dust off one of his boots.

"But I've talked to everyone who had any contact with Rachel at all - co-workers, dry cleaners, her hair stylist. They don't have a clue. I checked at hotels for any suspicious weekend bookings, like for a Mr. and Mrs. Smith, and I've come up dry. Whatever she was doing, she told no one."

"Come on, Enos," Lucian said in a sharp tone. "Surely you can do better than that. There's got to be someplace you're not looking."

"There's not." Enos leveled a hard look at Lucian.

"So you're just going to quit looking? Do I have to remind you how important this case is?" Lucian glared at Enos.

"Did I say I was going to quit?"

"You didn't have to. You obviously have." Lucian stood, his voice rising.

"If you think someone else can do better, feel free to find someone else for the job." Enos jumped to his feet and headed toward the door.

"Boys, boys," Mrs. Spicklemeyer said, appearing in the doorway and blocking Enos' exit. "We're all under a lot of stress. Now is not the time to take it out on each other."

Enos moved to go around her and she sepped in front of him, planting a palm on his chest. "Enos, please." Looking around him to lock eyes with Lucian, she said, "And you apologize. You know Enos has done everything he can. I don't think he's slept any more than you have in the past few months."

A beat of silence passed, and then Lucian spoke, his voice husky.

"I'm sorry, Enos. You're the best investigator I've ever seen. If you can't find the answer, no one can. I'm just..." he broke off, sinking back down into his chair.

"Aw, hell, Lucian. It's no big thing." Enos patted Mrs. Spicklemeyer's shoulder and then turned and walked back to his chair. She looked at them both as though to assure herself that the truce was permanent, and then disappeared from the doorway.

"Well," Lucian said, lifting his chin, his voice back to normal.

"I can still use that information. Even if I don't know where she was going or why, I can paint a picture of a woman going off to secret trysts, having to be so careful that she couldn't tell anyone. Everyone knows Rachel was the opposite of careful, so she wasn't doing it to preserve her own reputation. And she was man-crazed. She wasn't going off to some quilting society. The whole thing just screams 'married man'."

Enos nodded. "You have to admit, it was out of character for Rachel to keep anything a secret. She was an in-your-face kind of woman who didn't care what anyone thought of her. She seemed to delight in the bad girl persona. The fact is, the only reputation she had was a bad one."

"Right," Lucian said, sitting up in his chair. "So, the secrecy had to be at the behest of whoever she was seeing." He snapped his fingers. "That's my argument." He stood, pacing. "A girl with a spotty reputation and who'd never kept a secret in her life suddenly disappears for days on end and uncharacteristically tells no one where she's gone. It's just a small step from there to planting the idea of an affair in the jury's mind."

"She had to really be in love with the man to keep her mouth shut," Enos said.

"You're right," Lucian said, nodding. "And what's the common denominator of every affair in which the woman is in love with the married man?"

"She pushes him to leave his wife," Enos said.

"You just gave me my SODDI category." Lucian's face shown with excitement and relief. "A married man threatened with exposure is exactly the kind of person a jury could believe would kill Rachel if she threatened to go public."

CHAPTER SEVEN

Collywobbles: A weird feeling in one's stomach

My mouth fell open as I surveyed the clothes mosh pit that was my room. Piled sweaters, skirts and jeans flowed off of Rosamund's bed into a river of color swelling across the floor. Mismatched shoes bobbed along the wave of clothing. Despite my strict instructions to keep her stuff on her side of the room, the mess crept over into my area like some kind of virulent fungus. Most days I could live with it, but I'd told Rosamund at least twenty times that my parents were coming to town which meant that Swisbo would be conducting something close to a white glove military inspection. I didn't want to start off the weekend with an unhappy Swisbo.

I put my backpack down and scooped piles of shoes off the floor that had migrated to my side, flinging them on top of Rosamund's bed to create a miniature Mount Everest. She had more clothes than I'd had in my lifetime.

I bent for another load and felt a fingernail stab me in the back.

"Hey Weeny."

I looked up, taking in Rosamund's outfit. She'd gotten the whole college wardrobe thing wrong, or maybe right. She wore a white shirt, plaid skirt, and blue knit blazer, just like some stereotypical Catholic schoolgirl. Except the shirt was unbuttoned down to there, the skirt was the size of a hanky, and the blue knit blazer hugged her curves like only super expensive tailoring could.

"You do know that no one really dresses like that," I said.

"I do," she said, smirking. "Everyone seems to like it."

Yeah, everyone with a Y chromosome.

"So, I assume since I was relieved of guard duty you saw your precious Michael?" Rosamund said, sneering a little over the last two words.

"Uh huh." And as I said the words, I couldn't help it. A dreamy smile creased my face.

"Do you give him that same goofy look when you see him?"

I scooped up another pile of shoes.

"You are such a baby. You've got to keep a guy off balance. The minute he thinks he's got your full attention, the challenge is over. He'll move onto someone else."

Like I'm going to take advice from Rosamund. So what if she has the instincts of Mata Hari when it comes to keeping men panting after her. She's not exactly unbiased when it comes to me and Michael. I'd felt like a deer being stalked by a mountain lion ever since Rosamund had moved in posing as my roommate to be my bodyguard. This is what happens when your bodyguard used to be engaged to your boyfriend. I was pretty sure she wouldn't jump in front of a bullet for me.

Make that 100% positive.

"Could you try to keep your stuff on your side of the room? I'm sick of moving your crap around. My parents are coming, and since you're obviously not going to make any kind of effort to clean up, I at least want them to know that the mess is all yours."

"Neatness was never my strong point. If you'd let me bring Lorinda, we wouldn't have this problem."

"Can you honestly see a goblin fitting in around here?"

"Whatever. What's the big deal about cleaning up? Your parents aren't going to be here until tonight. We've got loads of time."

I noticed the "we" in her statement and tried to ignore it. "Samantha's parents are coming in a few minutes and I don't want them to think her suitemates are starring in some episode of *Hoarders: Buried Alive*."

"Who cares what they think? They're just hicks from nowhere."

"And then I'm going to lunch with them," I continued, as I threw a t-shirt and some kind of a hat over to Rosamund's side of the room.

"You're killing me here," Rosamund said, her face screwing up in a pout. "Aren't they farmers or something? This is going to be like Ma and Pa Kettle coming to town. I bet they'll show up in bib overalls."

"You don't have to go," I said, really, really wishing she wouldn't.

"You know I do. Michael would kill me if I didn't," she said, her mouth turning down a little.

I sighed, hoping that Rosamund wouldn't ruin the occasion. I'd been looking forward to meeting Samantha's parents, people apparently so cool that Samantha blew out of the dorm every Friday afternoon to rush home for the weekend. Much as I loved my parents, one reason I'd gone so far away to college was so I couldn't go home or be expected to go home on weekends. And, if I were honest, I don't think they want me to come anyway.

Win-win, sort of.

"And by the way," she said, turning her back on me and applying lip gloss using the full- length mirror on the wall, "if you think shoving that stuff onto my side of the room is going to get me to put it up, you're wrong."

Ergo the "we" in her earlier statement. Big surprise. I wondered if I could stuff everything into her closet. Absent a vacuum packer, I didn't think it would all fit.

I scooped up another pile of clothes and started to fling them onto Rosamund's bed when I felt something round and metallic graze my fingers. I grabbed it instinctively as the clothes arced through the air toward the bed.

A locket on a gold chain hung from my fingers with a heart etched onto it. I snuck a glance at Rosamund, but she was still preening in front of the mirror.

I felt for the catch, trying to get it open.

"When are the Children of the Corn getting here?" Rosamund said, glancing over her shoulder at me.

"Any minute," I said, clenching my fist over the locket.

"Yippee. I can't wait." She plopped onto her bed, watching me.

I bent and tucked the necklace under some clothes in my laundry basket. Okay, so I'm a snoop. But I just couldn't bring myself to trust Rosamund, and I never would've dreamed she'd be the kind to have a girly, romantic locket. Inquiring minds want to know and all that. I put the rest of my dirty clothes on top and shoved the basket into my closet.

I turned and caught a quick movement coming from Rosamund's direction out of the corner of my eye. Her eyes met mine, looking as wide and innocent as though she'd just gone to confessional and been absolved of all sins.

Which, of course, would never happen.

I peered at her bed and then I saw it, the edge peeking out from underneath her pillow where she must have shoved it. At that moment, I understand how a seemingly mild person about whom all the neighbors say "but he's such a lovely man, always edging my lawn for me" could have morphed into the axe murderer who'd chopped his live-in mother-in-law to bits. I wanted to strangle Rosamund.

I marched over to her bed and jerked my mother's logbook out from underneath the pillow. The leather volume is the only link I have to my real mother, and I've been poring over it every night trying to learn anything about her that I could. Knowing that Rosamund with her contemptuous attitude had been pawing through something so precious made me sick to my stomach.

"What are you doing with this?" I said, shaking the book at Rosamund.

"Don't get your panties in a wad," she said, unfazed. "There's nothing interesting in it."

"That's not the point and you know it. It's my property. You have no right to read it."

I carried the book over to my back pack, and what I saw as I slipped it inside turned the slow burn that had been building into a boiling rage. I whirled to face Rosamund.

"You dog-eared pages in it?" I couldn't have been more horrified if she'd desecrated a Bible.

"How else was I to keep my place? Certainly not by the content – your mother seems to have been as boring as you are," Rosamund said, picking up a file and working on one of her nails.

My hands fisted and I started toward her, ready to smack the smug look off her face.

"You really want to take me on?" She dropped the file and rose gracefully from the bed, a smile widening on her face.

A knock sounded on the adjoining door.

I stepped back, my eyes still locked on Rosamund.

"Ariel?" I heard Samantha's muffled voice through the door.

"This isn't over," I said, glaring at Rosamund.

"Anytime, anywhere," Rosamund said grinning.

I broke her gaze and tried to shove my anger down. I drew in a deep breath and then another. I pasted a smile on my face turned, and said, "Come on in."

Samantha opened the door, nudging a weathered-looking couple into the room.

"These are my parents," she said, beaming. "Mom, Dad – this is Ariel and," her smile dimmed a couple of watts, "Rosamund, my suitemates."

"I'm so glad to meet you both," Mr. Snelling said. "We always like getting to know Samantha's friends." His eyes widened at Rosamund's outfit, and he quickly looked away, taking in the room. I hoped he noticed that all the mess was on her side of the room.

"We're so happy to meet you too," Rosamund said, her voice syrupy sweet. "And where did you get that lovely suit Mrs. Snelling? I haven't seen that style in ages."

Samantha's eyes shot daggers at me. I snuck a glance at Mrs. Snelling. Uh oh. Her cheeks were red. Rosamund's sugar tone hadn't fooled anyone.

Until this moment, I'd thought Samantha's obsession with dressing like an extra on the *Partridge Family* t.v. show with her love beads and psychedelic blouses was totally random.

Turns out her mom is a frailer version of Shirley Jones, the actress who played the mom on the show. In fact, Mrs. Snelling wore what I could swear was an identical Mrs. Partridge purple velveteen suit with a ruffled shirt.

"I know it's a bit dated, but I've always loved purple and this was on special at the Co-op. I don't have a way with clothes like Samantha." One of Mrs. Snelling's small hands rubbed the lapel on her jacket, the worry wrinkle between her eyes deepening.

Rosamund choked. "Like – "

"You look just fine, mother," Mr. Snelling said, taking her hand from her lapel and holding it firmly with his tanned one. He looked like a rancher who'd been whittled down to the sinew by wind, worry and hard work. His face sprouted about twenty more wrinkles as he looked over at Mrs. Snelling.

"Thanks for inviting us to lunch Mrs. Snelling," I said quickly. "I didn't know anyone here when I came and Samantha has been a lifesaver."

She gave me a tiny smile but the red in her cheeks didn't fade.

"Rosamund and I need to check on one thing down the hall before we go," I said, grabbing Rosamund's wrist. "We'll be right back."

I pulled Rosamund out the door and down the hall.

"You're not coming with us," I said, my words coming out in a furious hiss. "You can't even be nice to Samantha's mother."

"I was nice," Rosamund said, smoothing her short skirt over her hips. "Believe me, I don't want to go with you but I'm on guard duty." She said it in an exaggerated tone, as if it were the worst chore in the entire world.

"Yeah right," I said, unable to help myself.

"What do you mean?" Rosamund said, eyes narrowing.

"Let's just say guarding me doesn't seem to be too high on your priority list. But if you insist on putting on a show of guarding me, then you can follow us in your car and watch from outside the restaurant. I'm not subjecting Samantha's parents to you," I said.

"I don't know what you're talking about," Rosamund said, her voice rising. "You're still alive aren't you? So no, I'll be right there by your side suffering through this ridiculous lunch with those small town hicks."

"No, you won't," I said, fighting to keep my voice down. "Because if you do, I'll tell Michael that you've been goofing off when you're supposed to be guarding me, surfing the net, and watching *The Real Housewives of Beverly Hills* when you should be following me to class. Not to mention snooping through my things. I don't think that will make him very happy."

Her face reddened. I hadn't been sure that she'd been watching t.v. instead of following me but I'd had my suspicions. Looks like I'd been right.

"Fine," she said. "But don't you ever threaten me again."

I tried to think of a zinger come back but one didn't come to mind.

"Whatever," I said.

That's the beauty of the word "whatever". You can use it whenever you're stumped for just the right put down, or for when you have the perfect one but would get beaten to a pulp if you actually said it.

We went back into the room and I informed everyone that Rosamund couldn't go. No one looked sorry.

Twenty minutes later, we were sharing a booth at Perkins Restaurant.

The waitress appeared at our table. "Ready to order?"

"You first, Mrs. Snelling," I said.

Samantha's mom shrank back into the booth as though I'd asked her to perform brain surgery.

"We'll both have the grilled cheese with fries," said Mr. Snelling.

"Me too." Samantha closed her menu with a snap.

Things went downhill from there. Mrs. Snelling didn't speak for the rest of the meal, Mr. Snelling spoke only when necessary, and Samantha was scarcely more vocal than her parents. A pall hung over the table.

I tried to fill in the gaps, but it didn't make a difference. I didn't know much about farming, which seemed to be all that Mr. Snelling was interested in, and no matter what conversational ball I threw to Mrs. Snelling, she missed it, as though I kept throwing her a greased-up football that was too slick to catch.

The lunch was a disaster.

CHAPTER EIGHT

Alexithyma:
Inability to identify or express one's feelings

he Snellings deposited us at the front door of the dorm, and I waved goodbye to their backs. Samantha was silent as we made our way up to her room. I followed her in, waiting for her to say something about the weird lunch.

Samantha flopped down on her bed.

The silence hung like a ten-ton weight.

"Samantha? Is everything okay with your mom?"

"Why?" Samantha's voice was sharp, defensive.

"Well, she didn't talk much at lunch. I just wondered..."

I didn't want to bring up how Mrs. Snelling hadn't ordered her own food. How she purposefully kept her eyes down most of the time. How Mr. Snelling never really seemed to take his eyes off her, not in an I'm-so-in-love-with-her way, but more like a watchful hawk. How Mrs. Snelling had looked at him for the okay to get up from the table.

Could it be possible that Mrs. Snelling was abused? That underneath that weathered exterior Mr. Snelling was a control freak wife beater?

"I mean, is everything okay with your parents? Do you need help on anything?"

"No." The answer was quick.

"Samantha, come on."

Samantha looked down, silent.

"Is something wrong with your mom? Or your dad?"

Still nothing.

"Is anyone," I paused, trying to think of a delicate way to say something horrible, "um, hurting your mother?"

"No." The word catapulted out of Samantha's mouth and she looked at me as though I had sprouted a horn in the middle of my forehead.

"Well, then what?" I said.

She picked at her nail polish and I grabbed her hands. "Now I know something's up. It took you hours to do your nails."

In keeping with her whole flashback to the 70's, Samantha had painstakingly painted both her finger and toe nails with peace signs – white with a pink background on her fingers, and a blue background outlining the symbol on her toes. I still couldn't figure out how she'd done it.

Samantha's eyes met mine and they were swimming in tears. Her mouth worked, and it took her a moment to get the words out.

"She has early onset Alzheimer's."

"Oh, no!" I sat down on the bed and hugged her. "Why didn't you tell me?"

"I don't know," she said in a thick voice, trying to hold back the tears. "I guess I just try not to think about it when I'm here. I've been going home every weekend to help my dad and just...just to see her. I know there will come a time when she doesn't remember me at all."

I stroked her hair, stunned.

"I just keep remembering this article I read about that the first female Supreme Court Justice? Sandra Day O'Connor? Her husband ended up not even recognizing her. He fell in love with another woman."

"I'm so sorry," I said, feeling like those were the three least helpful words in the entire world.

"That's why I dress like I do," Samantha said, brushing the tears from her face, and sitting up straighter. "My mom loves the *Partridge Family* – always has. Lately all she watches are old reruns of the show. My dad bought dvd's of the series, and just leaves them playing all the time. It makes her happy. Like she's creating a whole Partridge Family world."

"I kind of hope that if I dress like one of them it will imprint on her mind so maybe she'll remember me longer. Or at least put me in the show for when she doesn't remember who I am. And it makes me feel closer to her to wear the clothes she likes even when I'm here at school."

"I get it," I said, nodding. "I'd do the same thing."

"That's even why I drive a VW bug," Samantha went on. "The body hasn't changed that much so it looks like a car from that time period."

"But what makes it so hard is that, at least for now, she knows she's a little...off." Her eyes flooded with tears again. "Dressing like Mrs. Partridge makes her happy, and in our little town everyone is fine with it. I should have called my dad this morning and said something, but I didn't even think about it. And who knows what kind of a day they were having before they got here? She might not have wanted to wear anything else."

I sat silent, not knowing what to say.

"I hate Rosamund!" she said, pounding her fist on the bed. "She's worse than Kristin ever was."

"I know. Pot luck roommates are the worst," I said, feeling guilty.

I'd spread the story that my old roommate, Kristin, had left school to go marry some rich guy in Europe and that I'd ended up having a random roommate assigned to me to take her place. Samantha had no idea that Kristin was dead and Samantha was my bodyguard.

I heard a timid knock on Samantha's door.

"Can't you ask housing services for someone else? Anyone would be better than her," she said.

The knock came again, louder this time.

"I don't know how you can stand to be in the same room with her for over five minutes," Samantha raged.

"Hey, Samantha. I think someone's at the door."

"No, they're not," she said, turning pink.

The knock came again, this time so loud that the door shook.

I cocked an eyebrow. Samantha slowly slid off the bed and went to the door, opening it a crack.

"Come back later," she whispered. "Ariel's here."

I heard a male rumbling on the other side of the door.

"Because I'm not ready to tell her yet," Samantha whispered.

"Don't want to tell me what?" I walked over, pulled the doorknob from her hand and swung the door open.

"Todd?" I said, looking at my nerdy study partner in surprise. "What are you doing here? Did I forget a study meeting or something?"

"No, erm, well, not really," Todd said, looking uncomfortable.

I glanced from his reddening face to Samantha's pink one.

"What's going on?"

And then I got it. I just couldn't believe it.

"You two are together?"

"Yeah," Todd said, his face now almost purple. He reached out and took Samantha's hand.

"Why didn't you tell me? How long have you been together?" I felt a little betrayed. Todd and Samantha were my closest friends on campus and they'd kept this from me?

"We've been together almost a month," Samantha said, looking proud and guilty at the same time.

"We weren't totally sure how you'd feel about it," Todd said. "I mean, you and I...I mean, really, Ariel, it wasn't meant to be. You're cool and all but I realized you're not my type."

"I don't – " And then I stopped. The weird thing was that even though I had no interest in Todd romantically, I was a tiny bit miffed. Todd was my friend, my computer geek, but more than that he was always the guy who reassuringly seemed to want to date me. You know, the guy you don't want, but who makes you feel good because he wants you. I felt strangely adrift, like I'd lost my fall back guy.

"We'll always be friends, okay?" Todd said, walking over and squeezing my arm.

"Sure." I took a breath. "And I really am happy for you guys."

"It's cool, huh?" Samantha beamed at me.

"Very." And if Todd could make Samantha smile like that after the debacle we'd just lived through, then he was clearly the guy for her.

"So, are you going to meet Samantha's parents?" I said to Todd.

"Well," he said, avoiding my eyes, "I've kind of already met them."

"Oh, good. Did you see them earlier today?"

They gave each other a guilty look.

"Todd has gone home with me the last three weekends," Samantha said, pulling at a hangnail on her peace sign painted nail. "He's been a big help."

So Todd saying he couldn't do study groups on the weekends had nothing to do with his off-campus tech job.

I didn't know how to explain what I felt, but it wasn't good. Oddly, I wanted to cry, but thankfully not so much that I couldn't control it.

Maybe I had good reason to cry. My two closest friends on campus had been lying to me. *Cosmo*-reading Samantha would normally have been shouting that she had a boyfriend to the rooftops and camped in my room every night dissecting the relationship, just like she did with me and Michael. Did they really think they couldn't tell me?

And Samantha hadn't even told me about her mother.

I sighed inwardly. So, it turns out that I'm delusional. Here I thought Samantha and Todd were my close friends, but apparently they view me as a closer-than-average acquaintance but not quite a friend, someone you're willing to hang out with but wouldn't tell your secrets to.

"I'm really glad you know now," Samantha said. "It's been a hard secret to keep. I guess we should have told you earlier."

"No problem," I said, trying to mean it as I turned to leave. "I'll leave you guys to it. I mean, not to IT, but to, um, whatever you guys are going to do," I finished lamely.

I don't think they even heard me. Samantha's tears were gone, and she and Todd looked like they were in their own happy love bubble built for two.

I trudged out the door and stood in the hall, my eyes burning.

I recognized the feeling that was causing the prickling of tears behind my eyes. I'd felt it all my life. You could call it being the odd one out, the third wheel, the square peg trying to fit into a hole that someone had ensured was round, or simple loneliness, but none of those labels were quite right.

I knew I was feeling sorry for myself and probably overreacting. If Swisbo saw me now, the look on her face would say "suck it up, buttercup", although she'd never be so crass as to come right out and say it. One of her pointed looks would be enough.

Still, I couldn't stop the tears now coursing down my face. Let's see, maybe I could try distraction. What would be a good definition for the bereft feeling I had at this moment?

I pondered the question, and slowly my tears dried up. I finally came up with what I thought was a pretty good definition:

> An unwanted state of being alone due to personal defects that are hidden, either by delusion, ignorance, or extreme social unawareness, from the individual who is alone.

Then, drawing on the smattering of Latin I remembered from high school, I applied words to the definition: *ritus leprosi socialis involuntarium*, which, loosely translated, pretty much sums up the way I feel. So what if I was being a tad melodramatic. If I wanted to throw myself a pity party, I might as well make it a good one.

Ariel Robinson, the involuntary social leper.

CHAPTER NINE

Tohubohu:
Confusion

Sixteen Years Ago: Murder Trial, Day Three

he man watched the Lucian rise from the counsel table with studied coolness. A slight smile played at the edge of his mouth, as if he knew he'd scored points on his answers to the prosecutor's questions and had no fear of Lucian Castlewhite.

"Detective Murrow," Lucian said, "you claim that Rachel was murdered in a meadow a few hundred yards away from Hyalite Lake, is that right?"

"Yes."

"In fact, I believe you referred to it as 'the killing field'?"

"That's correct."

"And you concluded that Rachel had been murdered in that area because you found her blood there?"

"Right. As I said earlier, the blood was identified unequivocally as hers by the medical examiner," the detective said in a confident tone. He was young, but looked and spoke like a professional who'd been at his job far longer than his age suggested.

Lucian walked back to the defense table and picked up a piece of paper, scanning it as he walked back toward the witness stand.

"How much blood did you find?" Lucian said, his tone mild.

"It's hard to put a quantity on it," the detective said, shifting minutely in his seat.

"Humor me. Try," Lucian said in an unruffled tone.

"Again, it would be hard to say," the detective said, giving a conspiratorial sideways glance at the jury, as though he and everyone else knew that Lucian had asked for the impossible.

"Well, was it a gallon of blood?" Lucian said, his voice still gentle.

"No." The answer came quickly.

"A half a gallon?" Lucian shot back.

"Probably not," the detective said after a pause.

"Could it have been as much as a pint?"

"No." Detective Murrow's cheeks had taken on a red tinge.

"How about half a cup?"

The jury's heads swiveled back and forth between Lucian and the detective, as though watching a tennis match.

The detective glanced over to the prosecutor's table but apparently found nothing there of help. He breathed out heavily through his nose. "As I said, it's very hard to say."

"This," Lucian said, waving the paper in his hand, "is a crime scene report detailing what was found in the meadow where you claim Ms. Scarborough was killed. Do you need to look at it to refresh your memory?"

"No," the detective said, his eyes narrowing.

"According to this report," Lucian said, his voice now stern, "the amount of blood found at the scene was slightly less than two cc's. Is that your memory?"

"Yes," said the detective, looking sullen.

"So in this 'killing field'," Lucian said, exaggerating the words, "you found less than half a teaspoon of blood, about the amount you'd get from scraping your knee?"

"The rain probably washed the rest of the blood away," the detective said, lifting his chin.

A sound almost like a groan came from the direction of the prosecutor's table. Lucian turned away from the jury to hide the smile tugging at his lips.

"Rain?" Lucian said, composing his face into serious lines. "Is that what you said Detective Murrow?"

"Yes," the detective said, his eyes burning a hole through Lucian.

"What day did Rachel Scarborough disappear?"

"January 14."

"And when did you find 'the killing field'," Lucian said, making quote marks with his fingers.

"That evening."

"From an anonymous phone tip – right?"

"Right."

Lucian walked back to the defense table and exchanged the sheet of paper in his hand for another.

"I have here," he said, holding up the paper, "a historical record of the rainfall in Bozeman, Montana." He adjusted his glasses and peered at it. "It shows that there was no rain, snow, sleet or precipitation of any kind on January 14 or 15."

The detective stared at Lucian, his face now pale.

"Do you have any evidence that it did, in fact, rain on January 14 or 15?" Lucian said.

Detective Murrow again looked over to the prosecution table while the prosecutor studiously looked at the wall clock behind the witness stand. The detective dragged his eyes back to Lucian.

"Well," he said, clearing his throat, "it could have rained up at Hyalite Lake and not shown the rain in Bozeman. Hyalite is over 3000 feet higher in altitude than the city proper. This is Montana you know. You see rain in the higher elevations all the time that don't make it to the city." Detective Murrow's words came fast, as though they were on the run just like he was.

"So," Lucian said, speaking slowly, "your theory is that even though the records show that it was sunny and clear on both January 14 and 15, that rain did fall on this 'killing field' which washed away all but a small amount of blood."

"Yes," the detective said, nodding.

"And you reach that conclusion because it would be unlikely that the Defendant could kill Rachel and only spill a tiny bit of blood?"

"Yes." Detective Murrow's voice had become stronger, the old confidence starting to return.

"Now," Lucian said, consulting the paper in his hand again, "this record also shows that the temperature did not reach over five degrees Fahrenheit on January 14 or 15, so that if a stray bit of precipitation did fall, it would have been snow." He looked up at Detective Murrow. "Would you agree with me that you cannot have rain at a temperature of five degrees?"

Detective Murrow's face turned a vivid shade of red, almost darkening into purple. Seconds ticked by.

"Would you like the question repeated?" Lucian said as the silence lengthened.

"No," the detective said, almost hissing, "you cannot have rain at a temperature of five degrees."

"And likewise, if snow in any significant amount had fallen, it would have covered the small bit of blood that was found, correct?"

"I guess so." The detective spoke in the surly tone of a teenager caught sneaking into the house after curfew.

Lucian walked over to stand directly in front of the detective, giving him a hard stare.

"Isn't it true, detective, that only two cc's of blood was found because that was all the blood that was ever there to find?"

"Objection," the prosecutor jumped to his feet, looking relieved to have the chance to break up the vivisection of his witness. "Calls for speculation."

"That's okay," Lucian said before the judge could rule. "I think the jury gets the point."

Detective Murrow started to rise from his chair but Lucian raised his hand. "I've got some more questions, Detective."

The detective sank back into the chair, looking like a patient who'd just had a root canal only to be told that his wisdom teeth would also have to come out.

Lucian walked back to the defense table, studied his notes, and then turned back to Detective Murrow.

"How do you kill someone of our kind?" Lucian said.

"With either a light sword or by plucking their heart out," Detective Murrow said. You could almost hear the unspoken "Duh" in the tone of his voice.

"And only the light sword results in blood."

"Yes."

"So, because you found some blood, you concluded that Rachel Scarborough was killed with a light sword."

"That's correct. Although there is another scenario," Detective Murrow said.

"We'll get to that in a minute," Lucian said in a genial tone. "Now, did the Defendant have a light sword?"

"Of course he did," the detective said.

"Let me rephrase the question. Did you find any light sword allegedly belonging to my client?"

"No," Detective Murrow said. "I'm sure he hid it. He wouldn't leave it laying around for us to find, now would he?"

"You turned his house, office and car upside down looking for a light sword, didn't you?"

"Well, the term 'upside down' might be a little..."

"And you scoured the area around Hyalite Lake and never found the alleged murder weapon?" Lucian cut in.

"Yes, but there are any number of places the Defendant could have hidden it." Detective Murrow folded his arms.

"The truth is you've looked for months and haven't found it, have you?" Lucian's tone was that of a no-nonsense principal to a recalcitrant truant.

"Y-yes," Detective Murrow said, looking as though one of his wisdom teeth had indeed just been yanked out.

Lucian consulted his notes again and then looked up at the detective.

"Would you please refresh the jury's memory on who in our society is allowed to have a light sword in their possession?"

"Members of the armed guard, certain diplomats, and all royalty," Detective Murrow said.

"What is my client's profession, detective?"

"He's an attorney," the detective said, twisting his mouth as though the word tasted bad.

"He's not someone who would have been issued a light sword or even allowed to have one in his possession, isn't that correct?"

"That's true, but there's a pretty robust black market out there. Someone as smart as the Defendant could have easily obtained one."

Lucian sighed and turned to the judge.

"Your Honor, I object to everything Detective Murrow said after the words 'that's true' as speculation, and ask for an appropriate instruction."

"Sustained," the judge said before the prosecutor could respond and turned to the panel. "The jury will disregard everything the detective said after the words 'that's true' and will not consider it in any way in your deliberations in this case."

"In a nutshell, Detective," Lucian said, walking over to stand by the jury rail, "your theory, is that my client, who does not own a light sword, and who was never issued a light sword, killed Rachel Scarborough with a contraband light sword that he then managed to hide so effectively that your best detectives couldn't find it?"

"Our evidence shows," the detective said, squaring his shoulders, "that the Defendant murdered Rachel Scarborough. Period. We believe he did it with a light sword, but we also know he could have done it another way."

"Yes, you mentioned that before, detective. You seem anxious to get to that other theory. Why don't you go ahead and share it with the jury?"

Detective Murrow hesitated, as though sensing a trap but not sure what it was or how to keep it from snapping shut.

"Well," he said, "there could have been a struggle which resulted in a small amount of bleeding, thus accounting for the blood, and then the Defendant managed to pluck her heart out."

Lucian stood still, letting the detective's words sink in.

"Did you find any signs of a struggle where you found the blood?"

"No," the detective said, looking away.

"Did you find the shriveled remains of a heart?"

"No, but the Defendant could easily have taken that away with him and disposed of it elsewhere."

"But it was never found," Lucian said.

"No." Detective Murrow fidgeted in his chair.

"And when you examined the body, did you see scratches or cuts or any signs of a struggle which would have resulted in the shedding of blood?"

The detective stared at Lucian, as though not sure he'd understood the question.

"Detective?" Lucian said.

"There was no body," the detective said.

Lucian gaped at him, as though hearing this piece of news for the first time.

"No body?"

"That's right."

"So that's why we have these alternate theories of light sword versus heart removal. You're not only speculating as to the cause of death, you're speculating as to whether there was even a murder at all, aren't you?"

"We know she's dead," the detective said in a loud voice. "She has not been seen for months and there is no evidence that she left town."

"Come on, Detective. The reality is that the police and prosecutor rushed to charge my client with murder when, for all we know, Ms. Scarborough is alive and well and just decided to leave our community, isn't that true?" Lucian's voice thundered throughout the courtroom.

"She wouldn't have done that. Nobody does that." The detective looked at Lucian as though Lucian were insisting that the world was flat.

"You were here during the prosecutor's opening statement, weren't you?" Lucian said.

"Yes."

"Didn't you hear him describe Ms. Scarborough as young, immature, without family, behaving in a reckless way, treating relationships as disposable?"

"I'm not sure he put it quite like that," the detective said.

"Isn't that just the sort of person who could decide to leave without telling anyone?"

"Objection," the prosecutor said. "Calls for speculation."

"Sustained," the judge said.

"Isn't it true, Detective Murrow," Lucian continued, unfazed, "that Rachel Scarborough could turn up tomorrow, unharmed?"

"No, that's highly unlikely given the evidence we have."

"But you can't totally negate that possibility, can you, Detective?"

Detective Murrow's lips tightened into a thin line.

When no answer came, Lucian walked over to stand directly in front of Detective Murrow.

"Yes or no, detective. Isn't it possible that Rachel Scarborough is alive?"

"Anything is possible," Detective Murrow said through gritted teeth.

Lucian looked back at his notes, figuring this was the best he was going to be able to get out of the detective.

"I'm going to change the subject now to the alleged relationship between my client and Rachel Scarborough. How many times was my client seen with Rachel?"

"Twice." Detective Murrow said.

"And what were they doing on those occasions?"

"She was seen walking with him."

"And both of those times, she was walking with him as though leaving his law office."

"Yes."

"They were never seen together at a restaurant?" Lucian said.

"No."

"Never seen together at a movie?"

"No."

"Never seen together at a party?"

"No." Detective Murrow's responses had slowed. He edged forward on his chair.

"Never seen in public on anything resembling a date?"

"No."

"Have you interviewed anyone who said that Rachel and my client were involved in a romantic relationship?"

"Objection," the prosecutor said, rising to his feet. "Calls for hearsay."

"It doesn't go to the truth of the matter asserted, Your Honor. In fact, quite the contrary since we contend that there never was any romantic relationship between Ms. Scarborough and my client."

"I'll allow it," the judge said. "Overruled. Please answer the question, detective."

"No." The word left the detective's mouth as though pulled out with great difficulty by forceps.

"Isn't it true, detective, that this whole theory of a relationship is something that was cooked up by the prosecutor's office to try to come up with a motive to pin on my client?" Lucian's eyes had gone from golden brown to molten espresso.

"Absolutely not." The detective's voice was strong, but he didn't look at Lucian or the jury as he said the words.

Lucian looked over at the jury and shook his head as though to say, "Can you believe he just said that?"

"I have one more area of inquiry," Lucian said.

Detective Murrow no longer looked like the confident young man who'd taken the stand. He now looked like someone who'd rather be anywhere but in the courtroom.

"Did you make any effort to track Rachel's movements in the months before her alleged death?"

The Defendant cleared his throat loudly. Lucian did not look around.

"We did some investigation," Detective Murrow said.

"And didn't you find that..."

A loud crash interrupted Lucian. All eyes turned to the defense table, which now lay upended onto its side. A buzz rose from the spectators, and whispers of "did you see that" could be heard above the hum.

"Order!" The judge brought down his gavel. The crowd quieted. "Mr. Castlewhite, I will not tolerate this type of behavior in my court."

"Your Honor," Lucian said, cheeks pink. "Could I have a moment with my client?"

"It's time for a recess anyway," the judge said. "We'll convene again in twenty minutes. And if there are any more outbursts like that one, your client will have to watch this trial from his cell."

Lucian hurried over to his client after the jury had been escorted from the courtroom. He waited until the guards had righted the upended table and then sat down next to the Defendant.

"What is the matter with you? Have you lost your mind?" A vein bulged in Lucian's forehead.

"Why didn't you tell me you were going in that direction? I thought we agreed that you'd run every argument by me," the Defendant said, looking as angry as Lucian.

"Enos found out that Rachel was AWOL several times before her disappearance, and no one knows where she went or who she was with. He just told me last night so I didn't have a chance to tell you. She was obviously up to something. This gives us what we need. I'm going to – "

"No, you're not." The Defendant's voice echoed through the courtroom. Bystanders craned their necks, while deputies took a step toward the two of them.

"We're fine," Lucian said, waving them off. He turned back to the Defendant. "Calm down. What is the matter with you?" he said in a whisper.

"Lucian, you will not, repeat, will not, mention, or even hint at, Rachel's disappearances." The Defendant had lowered his voice, but his jaw tightened.

"You're clearly not thinking straight." Lucian's voice was tight with frustration. "As your lawyer, I'm telling you we need to go into her odd behavior in the months before her alleged death. The jury needs to hear it. We believe she was having an affair with a married man, and that's why she was so secretive. It gives us someone else to point to, the classic SODDI defense."

"Lucian," the Defendant said, staring him straight in the eyes with a fierceness that had Lucian leaning back as though to dodge a firebolt. "I will fire you right this second if you go any further. Not one more word on those absences.

"But – "

"I'll take over my own defense," he said, in a tone that could have shredded steel with its forcefulness. "Make no mistake, Lucian. I'll do it."

CHAPTER TEN

ALL-OVERISH:
FEELING VAGUELY UNEASY OR SLIGHTLY INDISPOSED

pushed open the door to my room to find Rosamund sitting at my desk with my laptop open. I'd worried that she might notice vestiges of tears on my face, but she barely looked up when I walked in. Apparently, she'd never had a computer of her own to just goof off on, and she was constantly checking tmz.com, radaronline.com, people.com, usmagazine.com, and any other gossip website she could find. She'd become obsessed with pop culture.

Her side of the room still looked like the aftermath of a 75% off store-wide Black Friday sale. Swisbo would have a fit.

"You do know that my parents will be here in a little while," I said.

"So?" Rosamund said, not looking up.

"So..." My voice trailed off. Hang on a minute. One look at

Rosamund's cyclone-struck side of the room, and Swisbo would deliver either a direct verbal smackdown in a pseudo-polite tone, or an exaggerated stare at the mess, coupled with a moue of distaste. Rosamund wouldn't let that slide.

It would be the equivalent of a black mamba facing off against a rattlesnake. I wondered if I had time to go get some popcorn for the show.

"Nothing," I said.

"So, how was your lunch?" Rosamund said. "It looked scintillating from my view on the street. Samantha's parents seem like a laugh riot." Her tone was snide.

I ignored her, retrieving the logbook from my backpack, and pulling my laundry basket from the closet.

"I'm going down to the laundry room," I called over my shoulder as I headed out into the hall and toward the elevators.

I hit "B" for Basement, and minutes later muscled my overflowing basket onto the nearest table. Note to self: do laundry more than once a month. This was going to take forever. I pulled some of the clothing off the top and something clinked to the tabletop. Rosamund's necklace. I'd almost forgotten about it.

I picked it up, found the catch and opened it to the picture inside.

I dropped it as though it were a tarantula. It lay open on the floor. I didn't pick it up.

Staring up at me from inside the locket was a picture of Aaron, Michael's brother. The one who'd murdered his own parents, the one who'd joined the Enemy, the one who'd threatened to kill my little brothers, the one who'd almost killed Dr. Fielding.

My brain moved with all the speed of a snail plowing through a trail of molasses. I'd never liked Rosamund. I'd suspected her of wanting to twist my arms off because of Michael, but I'd never once suspected this.

My bodyguard was working with the Enemy.

I leaned against the laundry table, my heart racing. Maybe there was some rational explanation for the picture. After all, she had been engaged to Aaron at one time, so maybe she stilled loved him.

However, she'd glommed onto Michael with the speed of a hungry cheetah going after the last antelope left in sub-Saharan Africa, and was so hateful to me you'd think Michael had been the love of her life.

Or maybe she was with Aaron, had always been with Aaron, and stayed behind to be a spy like Achimalech, deliberately cozying up to Michael to be close to the seat of power.

But Michael always took up for her, trusting her so much that he'd made her my bodyguard. Could he be that wrong?

No way. He'd known her forever.

But then again, he'd known Achimalech forever and look how that turned out.

My head started to throb. I speed dialed Michael. Straight to voice mail.

Of course.

I tried to talk myself down from the cliff. So Rosamund had a picture of Aaron. He had been her first real love, so it was natural that he'd have a special place in her heart. On the other hand, he'd betrayed everyone, including her, so you'd think she'd want to burn every picture she had of him.

Or maybe this was an old necklace from back when she and Aaron were engaged that she'd forgotten about. But then why would she bring an old necklace with her to my dorm?

I had to talk to someone.

I dialed Barnaby. Maybe he could get Michael to come to the phone.

"What's the shizzle dizzle?" came the raspy voice through my phone.

"Hey Barnaby. I've ...."

"Hold on. Let's Face Time, okay?"

The line went dead.

I stared at my phone, and then it lit up with Barnaby's call. I answered, and his pumpkin-shaped face filled the screen.

"So rad, right? It's just like we're in the same place." His globular eyes almost popped out of his head with excitement.

"I've been trying to reach Michael but he's not answering. Is he around?"

"And how are you, Barnaby? How's your life going? What, have I turned into just your go-between to Michael?" He glared at me.

"Sorry, Barnaby," I said. "I'm just a little wigged out. Guess whose picture is inside Rosamund's locket?"

"I guess you don't think someone like me could have a personal life with super cool things happening in it. The world revolves around more than just one person, you know."

"But..."

"I've got things going on too. Do you ever ask me about them? Nope. It's just Michael this and Michael that and where is Michael and when is Michael coming over and do you know what Michael is doing." His voice was aggrieved.

I felt a twinge of guilt. I wasn't quite as bad as Barnaby claimed, but, since Michael never seemed to have his phone with him, Barnaby did field a lot of Michael GPS inquiries from me.

"I'm sorry Barnaby. I just wanted to..."

"And that's the problem. It's always what you want. What about what I want?"

Okay, this was over the top even for Barnaby. His eyes glistened, and his chin, improbably small on his wide head, actually quivered.

"What's wrong?"

"It's nothing." He swiped a hand across his eyes.

"Come on, Barnaby, what is it?"

He said nothing, and a single tear rolled down his cheek.

"Oh Barnaby." A wave of dread passed over me. Had something terrible happened? I'd never seen Barnaby so upset. "Please tell me."

"You'll think I'm silly." I relaxed. Maybe it wasn't something dire after all.

"No, I won't, I swear."

"Do you..." he looked down so that I could only see the top of his head. He cleared his throat. "Do you think I'm hot?" His voice shook.

"Hot? Like..." I hesitated, not sure what he was asking.

"You know, like a hottie." His face filled the screen again. "Like a babe magnet, a GQ, a McDreamy, a cutie-patootie, a sexy beast, a stone-cold fox, a..."

I held up my hand. "I got it. Why are you asking?"

"Am I or not?" His chin jutted forward.

I thought fast. Barnaby certainly didn't fit the standard definition of someone to swoon over. On the other hand, he's a goblin, and I'm no expert on goblin attractiveness.

There are times for fibs and times for truth. This was definitely a fib time, but I wasn't sure I could carry it off.

"Here's what I think," I said, trying to sound sure, like Barnaby's hotness factor was something I'd pondered and had formed definite opinions about. "There are two categories of attractive guys – cute guys and sexy guys. Both categories are great. And, if you start dating a cute guy, they become a sexy guy in your eyes. And no matter how anyone looks at first glance, if you get to know them and start having feelings for them, they become sexy to you. Personally, I prefer cute guys."

Barnaby's tears stopped.

"Sexy guys are too intimidating. And sexy fades, while cute lasts. I think you're a cute guy. Endearingly cute. Adorably cute. Devastatingly cute."

That was no lie, at least the part about Barnaby being cute. He reminded me a bit of a pug puppy – not traditionally handsome but endearingly appealing.

I hoped Barnaby wouldn't catch the lie that I did tell. The one about preferring cute guys. Michael definitely did not fall into the "cute" category.

Barnaby's eyes brightened.

"Really?"

"Yes, really. So, now tell me why you want to know."

His face reddened and he lowered his gaze to the floor again. My screen showed only the top of his bald head, which looked a bit like a wide, greenish-scarlet tomato.

He mumbled something.

"What?"

"I mumble mumble. She's the mumble."

"Barnaby, you're going to have to speak up or at least look at me. I can't understand what you're saying."

He raised his head, looking abashed.

"I really like Lorinda."

Ah. Things were starting to make sense.

"Have you asked her out?"

"No, 'cause see I thought she was with Zeke, but I heard from Benny who talked to Ezra who dates Esther that she saw Zeke holding hands with Deborah so the word is that they must be kaput."

"Sounds like the coast is clear. Why haven't you asked her?"

"Duh." He looked at me like I'd flunked a basic IQ test. "Lorinda is the bomb. I mean she's fine - a real babeshow. And Zeke had hair." Barnaby rubbed his own bald head. "I don't think she'd go out with someone like me."

"Barnaby." I shook my head. "You're about to be Head Doorkeeper. You're the funniest, smartest goblin on the Mountain. She'd be nuts to turn you down."

"I don't know." Barnaby's mouth turned down.

"How well do you know her? Are you guys friends?"

"Not really. We've only spoken a few times, but she smiled at me today."

"Why don't you just ask her out to do something casual?" I

racked my brain. What do goblins do for casual outings? For that matter, what do goblins do on pull-out-all-the-stops dates?

"Something casual?" Barnaby's huge brow wrinkled.

"You know, like what you do in your free time, for fun."

His face fell. "She wouldn't like that."

"What do you mean?"

"You know." He gave me an aggrieved look. "Gaming. The only thing I really do in my free time is play games. *League of Legends, Overwatch* – those kind of games. I don't know anyone else that does that. None of the other goblins even use a computer. When I talk about it, everyone just looks at me like I'm some kind of fruit loop."

"That's probably because they don't know what you're talking about. It's pretty cool that you're computer savvy. That's a plus, not a minus."

He looked dubious.

"She'd probably be fascinated."

"But what if she's not?" Barnaby said.

"Then you'll find something else. Or, you might decide she's not what you're looking for if she's not interested in technology."

"Never happen. She's the one," he said, shaking his head.

"Then I guess you're going to have to ask her out."

"But what if she says no?"

"What if she does? What's the worst that could happen?"

"It'd be an epic smackdown. I'd be roadkill. You know, like a squirrel that's been run over 100 times, smashed flat, and has flies crawling all over it."

I swallowed, trying not to think about the picture he'd just drawn.

"And what if you don't ask her out?"

"I guess," he paused, "I guess I'll never know if she likes me."

"So which is worse?"

"You're a big help." He scowled at me.

I grinned at him. "So now that we've talked about your problem, can we talk about mine?"

"Fine." He blew out a sigh. "What is it?"

"Rosamund has a locket."

"Rosamund has a locket? I'd never have figured her for the lovey-dovey sentimental type."

"Right? But she does. And it's got Aaron's picture in it."

"Whoa. That's some serious sick slam-o-rama."

"I've never trusted her."

"Yeah," Barnaby nodded. "You and Rosamund would give the Hatfields and McCoys a run for their money. But, it could be something from back in the day, when they were together."

"It could, but why would she have it with her in my dorm room? You'd think it would be buried in a sock drawer, or burned, or dipped in acid or something. I mean, supposedly Aaron left her, and she doesn't strike me as the forgive and forget type."

"I know, baby doll. This one's a head scratcher. Maybe we should ask Michael."

I almost banged my head against the wall. "Yes, Barnaby, I think we should. So can you get him?"

"No can do. Strict DND orders."

"DND?"

"Do not disturb. According to the Doorkeeper Handbook, that means I can't disturb him unless the world is ending, the Enemy has launched an attack, a rebellion has broken out here at Headquarters or..." He paused. "Dang it! I forgot the fourth one!" He disappeared from the screen and I heard pages flipping. He bobbed back onto my phone screen. "Or there is an imminent threat to his life."

Barnaby was really taking this whole Head Doorkeeper thing too seriously.

I puffed out a breath. "Surely there is some exception for girlfriends."

"Nope. I'll tell him to call you as soon as he gets out of his meeting, sugar pop."

"When will that be?"

"Rule 42.1 says I can't give out any intel about Michael's schedule. For security reasons."

"You've got to be kidding."

"Nope. Unless you're a blood relative or a spouse, a form 42.1(b) must be filled out and signed by Michael designating you as a person with whom his schedule can be shared. No such form has been filed." He sounded pompous.

I wanted to reach through the phone and wring his green neck.

"Michael probably doesn't even know he's supposed to fill out a form like that. You know he wouldn't have a problem with telling me his schedule."

"Maybe so baby-o but that's not my problemo."

"So I guess under those rules, you could tell Aaron what his schedule is since he's a blood relative." My voice was scornful.

Barnaby's brow furrowed into two ridges.

"Right?" I said.

"Give me a minute," he said, squinching his eyes shut in thought.

"Barnaby!" His eyes snapped open. "This is serious. Rosamund has a picture of one of the Enemy, the guys who want to take the Piece of Home away from me, in a heart shaped locket. Not to mention the fact that he's the same guy who killed Michael's parents. And she's my bodyguard, the one who's supposed to protect me from the Enemy. Don't you think Michael would want to know that right away?" I glared at the screen.

"Don't get mad at me," he said, his face falling. "No goblin has ever held this job, and I don't want to screw up. I mean, I swore to 'faithfully uphold and attend to all the rules, regulations, duties and responsibilities' of the Head Doorkeeper. The rules say I can't tell you when he'll be out of the meeting and I can't interrupt him."

I sighed. This scenario had probably never come up before, or at least not for ages. Achimalech had not been married and, as far as I knew, hadn't had a girlfriend. The mere thought of him and a girlfriend creeped me out. The previous ruler, Michael's father, had been married. I'd have to talk to Michael about the rules.

"It's okay, Barnaby," I said. "I'm sorry I lost my temper. It's just that Aaron scares me to death, and the fact that Rosamund might be on his side..." My voice trailed off.

"I can't imagine that she is," Barnaby said. "I know you two haven't hit it off, but she's always been loyal."

"I'm sure that's what they said about Aaron before he...did what he did." I couldn't bring myself to say the words "murdered his parents" out loud.

"That shocked the you-know-what out of everyone," Barnaby said, nodding. "But, he was always off the hook. If you told him to go right, he went left. And always pulling tricks on everyone. Like the time we had the international conference of the Descendants here. We had all the muckety-mucks from all the different divisions of the hemisphere here and Aaron managed to release thousands of horse flies at the final banquet. They stung the guests, landed on the food. It was actually kind of funny to see everyone in their robes running for cover, but his parents were not amused."

"That sounds like just a prank."

"Yeah, in the beginning they were pranks. But then he got all surly-like, and the pranks got way outta hand. And then two days before the murders, we found all these dead cats right outside the main entrance to Headquarters. They'd been strangled, and his initials were carved into their stomachs. His mother loved cats. She couldn't believe he'd done that."

"You're kidding." My stomach rolled. Killing animals was a cardinal sign of a psychopath. I knew that from watching *Law and Order, Criminal Intent* reruns.

"He swore he didn't do it, but we all knew he did. People think that's why he killed his parents. The rumor was that they were talking about sending him away to his relatives in the Southern Hemisphere, and everyone figured he just went Rambo on them."

I heard the faint sound of a gong and Barnaby jumped. "Gotta go puddin'pop. They're calling."

"Tell Michael..."

The phone screen went black.

I blew out a sigh and turned back to my basket. Neither rain nor sleet nor snow nor the possibility that my bodyguard really does want to kill me could change the fact that I had to get my laundry done before Swisbo arrived. Spotting a full laundry basket would give rise to a lecture on procrastination and what an unlovely character trait that is. There'd be enough mine fields to navigate over the weekend, and I wanted to at least start the visit in the plus column.

I finished unloading my clothes, dutifully separating whites, darks, and delicates into adjoining machines, added laundry soap and started them up. Then I stopped. I'd been concentrating so hard on the Rosamund problem that I hadn't noticed that the laundry room and all the machines in it were empty except for my clothes.

Odd. Usually I was lucky to snag one washer at a time. Maybe I was the only one who had to do laundry before my parents arrived.

I hoisted myself up onto the laundry table, legs dangling over the side, and cracked open my bio-mom's leather logbook. I inhaled its scent, a paradoxical cross between stale dust and exotic adventure. So far, though, its contents had been more on the dusty side of things. Golgoran had told me my bio dad was still alive, a thought which filled me with hope and broke me out in a cold sweat at the same time, and I'd hoped to find some clues as to his identity as well as some personal details about my bio mom. No luck. I'd resigned myself to reading the whole thing word by excruciating word, a task almost worse than calculating the limit as *x* approaches negative infinity of the square root function.

Yeah, that tough.

The woman had never heard of double spacing. She filled every line, margin to margin, as though paper were still made from papyrus by enterprising monks and available only after bribing the abbot to be moved up on the paper waiting list.

And paragraphs? She'd apparently given them up for Lent one year and decided never to use them again. Sometimes I had to read several sentences before figuring out that she'd changed topics.

Thankfully, my eyes would get a break every three of four pages when she drew sketches, either of relics she'd found, or what looked like terrain with various measurements penciled in. Then, and only then, did she allow some precious space between items.

Reading the thing felt like water torture, the drip, drip, drip of deciphering one crabbed sentence after another beating me down. And then there were all these symbols that I didn't understand. Some were chemical symbols, while others I couldn't begin to make sense of.

One night I'd gone to the trouble to look up $(Ca,Na)_2$ $(Mg,Fe,Al)_5(Al,Si)_8O_{22}$ $(OH)_2$ which turned out to be the composition of Hornblende, which, upon further research, I discovered was "a calcium-rich amphibole mineral that is monoclinic in crystal structure", the primary component of the metamorphic rock which makes up the bottom of the Grand Canyon.

I felt a little glow knowing that my bio-mom was on a first chemical name basis with rocks. We had at least one thing in common besides DNA. I've loved rocks since I was a kid. I'd had a rock polisher that could turn common gravel into striated glowing bands of color.

But I really wanted to know about my father, and some personal details about my mother. I wasn't getting much out of the dry Sahara that was my mother's logbook.

However, I wasn't going to quit. No matter how boring, awful or incomprehensible, I've never been able to quit reading a book until I'd finished it, and this logbook was no different. I'm obsessive that way.

Hmmm. Pot/kettle?

A loud buzz sounded and I dropped the book. Two others

followed. I whirled and then shook my head. It was the just the washing machines. Get a grip!

As I transferred the clothes to the dryers, I heard a muffled thud. I turned, looking around the room. Nothing.

I shook my head. The uncharacteristically empty room was giving me the willies. I tried hard not to remember all the horror movies where people were tortured and killed in basements. You know, *Silence of the Lambs, The Return of the Living Dead, Don't Breathe*....

Stop it! I gave myself a mental slap. Those were f-i-c-t-i-o-n. Millions of homes have basements. Mega millions have laundry rooms. They're just normal, every-day rooms.

And then I felt it. That preternatural sense I get before I'm transported, as though my cells were already shrinking from the ordeal.

Before I could scream "No-o-o-o-o", I felt myself ripped away, the force of the transport drilling my eyes shut. I spun, catapulting through black air. Then my head exploded in terrific pain.

CHAPTER ELEVEN

SHANGHAI: TO SNATCH, KIDNAP

I heard voices coming from somewhere far away.

"You killed her." The voice was raspy.

"No I didn't," said a squeaky voice.

"Yes, you did. Man, are you in trouble," Raspy said.

"But it wasn't my fault." Squeaky sounded almost frantic.

"Doesn't matter. I've got the instructions right here."

I heard rustling sounds as though someone were unfolding a sheet of paper.

"Maimin', cuttin', gorin', burnin' and amputatin' are perfectly acceptable so long as they don't result in death."

"But I didn't do any of those things!" Squeaky said.

"Same difference. You whapped her head on the floor when we landed."

"It doesn't say anything about not hitting her head."

"You're missing the point you idiot. The gist of this is that we're not supposed to kill her," said a third voice.

"C'mon Frankie. It doesn't say that," said Squeaky.

"Well, I wouldn't want to be you trying to explain to you know who how you thought these orders meant it was okay to kill her so long as you didn't do it by maiming, cutting, goring or amputating," said the man I now knew to be Frankie.

No one said anything for a moment.

"But it was an accident," said Squeaky, sounding terrified.

"Yeah, like that'll fly. I wouldn't wanna be you," said Raspy.

I heard the door open.

Footsteps came toward me. I kept my eyes shut. Maybe if I played possum they – whoever they was – would leave me alone.

The footsteps stopped right next to my ear. A second later, I felt a breath on my face. Goosebumps pricked my arms.

A hand gripped my arm and jerked me to a sitting position. My eyes flew open.

I'd give anything to have kept them closed. I looked straight into familiar shark eyes, mesmerized. They didn't reflect light. It was like looking into an abyss, but I couldn't break the gaze. I shivered.

"Hello Ariel," Golgoran said.

The one time I'd met Golgoran he'd scared the crap out of me, and that was before I'd learned he's the Chief Enforcer for the Enemy. You know, the go-to guy when you need to get something out of someone who doesn't want to give it to you, like Paulie on *The Sopranos*.

Once, when Swisbo thought I was getting too enamored with *The Sopranos*, she made me write a report on Mafia hitmen. Yes, this does seem like a weird assignment from one's own mother, but I never watched the show with the same fervor after that. The woman is a genius.

There was Kid Twist Reles, who killed over a thousand people in the '30's and '40's, usually by ramming an icepick through their brains. Mad Sam DeStefano didn't kill as many people as Kid Twist, but he loved to torture his victims and actually had his own soundproof basement to "play" in. And don't forget Dasher Abbandando, who preferred a meat cleaver to more civilized forms of killing.

I'm just spit-balling here, but I'm betting that some mob members get squeamish about actually breaking legs or pulling off fingernails, which is why they launder money or run the strip clubs, while people with names like "The Animal" Barboza are tasked with killing people.

I can't really imagine evil beings, actual demons, losing their lunch over torturing someone. That's why I couldn't catch my breath. The thought that if, like Golgoran, you're an actual enforcer in the Enemy's organization, you must be cruel on an unimaginable level. In other words, wired like a T-Rex who'd slept the night before on a particularly rocky bed, hasn't eaten in days and knows extinction looms unless it kills every living creature in sight and claws out all their internal organs for food.

I wheezed, trying to grab some oxygen. I was in the same room with possibly the most sadistic creature in the universe and no cavalry waited around the corner to rescue me. Whatever "perimeter" had been around me, they'd gotten through.

And Rosamund...I guess I had my answer. She'd betrayed me. She'd been with the Enemy all along.

"Hey, boss. She's turning blue," said Frankie.

"I...can't...breathe," I said.

"All she's doin' is breathin'," said Raspy.

"Frankie, get a paper bag," Golgoran said.

I felt a sack pressed against my mouth. For a second I wondered if you could die from fright. It had to be better than suffering a painful death at Golgoran's hands. But a hand held the back of my neck and jammed the sack tight against my lips. My breathing finally slowed. The hand tightened around my neck, jerked my head up and shoved me into a chair.

"Feeling better?" Golgoran said, eying me with those bottomless black eyes.

I sat in a tufted chair with wooden armrests facing a walnut desk. I squinted at it, wondering if my aching head was playing tricks on me. The desk was covered with ornate carvings except for one smooth space in the middle of the top. It looked like the furniture equivalent of someone who'd covered every inch of his body except his face with tattoos. But that wasn't the weird part. The desk rippled with movement, almost making me seasick.

Golgoran walked around the desk and sat down in a high-backed leather chair. He wore pin-striped pants, a starched white shirt and navy blue suspenders. His suit coat hung over the back of the chair and the silver cane I remembered from our first meeting leaned on the side of his desk. He looked at me as though I were the cause of all the trouble in the world.

I swiveled to look at Squeaky, Raspy and Frankie standing behind me, thinking anything would be better than looking at Golgoran. They looked fairly normal until you made eye contact. It was like being surrounded by hyenas already fantasizing about foraging among the remains of my body.

I put the paper bag back up to my mouth.

"Everybody leave," Golgoran said.

"But boss, she's the one who..." Raspy said.

"Out."

"But she might..." Frankie started and stopped when Squeaky jabbed him with his elbow.

"I can handle a little girl," Golgoran said, his voice a harsh rasp.

"It's not that," said Frankie, holding his hands out as though trying to tame a fractious lion. "Really. We just want to be close in case you need us. You won't even know we're here."

"I. Don't. Need. You." Golgoran said the words through clenched teeth, glaring holes into all three.

They stared back at him but didn't move.

"Go," Golgoran shouted and with one swift move picked up his silver cane and threw it like a javelin straight at Frankie, hitting him in the chest like a dart thrown at a bull's eye.

Frankie stared at Golgoran, his eyes goggling so far out of his head that he looked for an instant like a cartoon character. He stared down at the cane and then sank to the floor in agonizing slow motion. Seconds later he lay still, eyes wide, his face wearing an expression of horrified astonishment.

Squeaky and Raspy gawked at Frankie. Golgoran made a sudden move toward them and they turned and ran, slamming the door behind them.

I heard what sounded like a yip from under the desk. Golgoran bent and reappeared holding something small, tan and fuzzy in his arms.

"It's okay baby girl," he said, stroking it. "I know you hate loud noises. It was just a door."

I peered at the bundle. It raised its head to be scratched and I took in the pink bow holding a tuft of hair on top of its head.

"Is that a...a...Yorkie?"

Golgoran nodded and, still holding the dog, walked over to Frankie and jerked on the cane. It came out with a *schwunk,* pulling out a black mass through the hole it had made in Frankie's chest. Gologoran flicked his wrist and what used to be Frankie's heart flew through the air, landing in the far reaches of the room and rolling to a stop in the corner.

I tried to squelch the panic flooding my body.

If Golgoran would do that to one of his own, what was he going to do to me?

CHAPTER TWELVE

Argle-bargle: A vigorous discussion

Wiping the end of the cane with a handkerchief, Golgoran strode back to his desk, plopping into his chair and settling the dog on his lap. Then he just sat there, stroking the Yorkie's ears.

Seconds passed. I clenched my hands into fists to stop the shaking. I couldn't take the silence anymore.

"What's her name?" I said, trying to sound normal.

"Tabitha."

"She's very pretty," I said, and then cleared my throat. What was I doing making chit-chat with someone who works for the devil? I couldn't just talk to him like a regular person, could I?

"Isn't she?" He stroked her, smiling, the picture of a proud father. "I got her from a breeder in Maine. Her father won the toy category at Westminster."

"She's an unusual color," I offered, lobbing the conversational ball back to him.

"Oh, yes. She's called a parti Yorkie because she has black, tan and white, whereas most Yorkies are just two colors, either black and gold, blue and gold, blue and tan, and black and tan. It's harder to find a well-bred parti-colored Yorkie." He adjusted the pink bow securing Tabitha's topknot. "The breeder didn't want to sell her, but I persuaded him."

I hated to think what the persuasion involved. "Are you going to breed her?" I said.

"Oh no. I don't want to put her through that," he said, "do I, my precious girl?" he added in a baby voice and kissed the top of Tabitha's head.

My mouth dropped, but before I could say anything else I was distracted by the carnage erupting on Golgoran's desk

Tiny carved gargoyles came to life, pushing and shoving each other. One tore the arms off of another as easily as plucking wings off of a fly. Undaunted, the now armless urchin head-butted him. I turned my head to the far corner of the desk only to see a chubby beast gouge an eyeball out of hapless imp and lick it. I stifled another gag.

I ripped my eyes away from the writhing creatures embedded in the desk, catching Golgoran's face in the corner of my eye. He'd stopped fussing over Tabitha, and had lifted his head to face me.

Huh? I looked at him full on.

The Golgoran I'd met before had been confident and in control. Sure, he'd been scary, overly chatty, slick and intense, but he'd looked and acted like everything was manageable by a mere flick of his pinky. A stereotypical baddie.

This guy looked about to jump out of his skin. The always immaculate Golgoran had a sheen of sweat on his upper lip, and his hair looked like it could use a cut. Lines radiated from his eyes and around his mouth that I hadn't noticed before. His hand trembled as he scooped another handkerchief out of his desk drawer and put it in his pocket. He put Tabitha down on the floor and she ran over to a tiny red velvet bed behind his desk.

"There's nothing in the world I'd like more than to kill you, Ariel." His voice was casual, as though he were discussing the weather.

So much for normal conversation. I'd been so distracted by his slackened sartorial standards that I'd forgotten to be afraid for a minute.

"It might even be worth the repercussions." He rose and paced slowly behind his desk, his hands clenching and unclenching under his frayed cuffs.

As the silence wore on, I started to shake. Waiting to hear what he was going to do to me was almost worse than hearing it.

I tried to think up nicknames for him to distract myself. This is one of my favorite games, and works like a charm when I'm nervous or scared.

Let's see, every mob killer had a nickname – "Drive-By" Corrado or "The Oven" Henning" or "Icepick" LeRow.

"What's your favorite way of killing people?"

"What?" He looked startled.

Had I actually said that out loud?

"N-nothing," I said.

"Did you ask how I kill people?"

I couldn't make my tongue move.

"Speak up." His face brightened, as though I were dull student who'd surprised him by remembering the mathematical number for π to the eighty-sixth digit.

"Just," I said, the word coming out in a whisper. I cleared my throat and tried again. "Just whether you have a particular signature to your, um, killings."

"No one has ever asked me that question before." He squinted at me, as if trying to figure out whether I was serious or just trying to butter him up.

Yeah, I couldn't imagine it coming up around the dinner table or at the supermarket. More to the point, I couldn't imagine Golgoran having any friends to shoot the breeze with, where they'd talk about stuff like how their day went, or the new guy at work, or how to most effectively slice and dice a human being in record time.

"But yes, I did have unique way of taking lives, which I worked on for a long time. I don't think anyone else did it quite like I did." He sat down, his face relaxing. He almost looked pleasant.

"See, I haven't actually killed someone in a long time."

"But you just did," I said before I could help myself.

"And here I thought you were a words person," he said, his tone condescending. "So much for your one talent."

I gaped at him, stung, and yes, a little angry. I am a words person. It's the only thing I feel almost confident enough to brag about.

"The definition of 'someone' is 'some person'," he said in a pedantic tone. "Frankie is one of our kind, so my statement was totally accurate. I haven't killed a human being in, oh, let's see, at least five hundred years. I have people for that. And my people have people for that."

"First of all, the definition for 'someone' is not limited necessarily to 'persons'," I said, my voice heating up. I straightened in my chair. "Second, how can you quibble over the definition of 'someone' when you just used the word 'people', which does, in fact, by definition mean human beings, as distinguished from animals or extra-terrestrial creatures? If you're going to require others to use the absolute definition of the word, then you need to be more careful in your own choice of words."

Whoops. I clapped my hand over my mouth. What was I thinking, arguing with a stone-cold killer, who, by the way, just happened to work for Satan? Maybe I was as stupid as Golgoran seemed to think I was.

Golgoran glared at me, and then waved his hand, the verbal

equivalent of "whatever". I guess even bad guys run out of good come-backs once in a while.

"Back in the day, my favorite way to kill people," he said, stressing the word, "was to drill a hole in their head, stick a custom-made tool in through the hole, swirl it around, and then suck the brain matter out."

My stomach lurched.

"Oh no, I don't mean I sucked it out and drank it," he said, seeing my discomfort. "I'm not a vampire. I hung them upside down, inserted a tube which acted as a siphon, started the siphon with a little suck, kind of like siphoning gas from a car tank, and then emptied it into a bucket. After the last drop drained out, I'd seal the hole and have a field day watching some medical examiner in some podunk city try to figure out why my victim didn't have a brain."

The skin on my scalp shrank.

"It really is an art," he said, his face softening as though reminiscing about a particularly pleasant vacation. "You have to find the best part on the scalp – if they have a mole that's helpful. And then you take a skosh of skin from between their toes to cover it up, preferably between the little toe and the one next to it."

If he was waiting for me to say something congratulatory, I just didn't have the words. I was still trying to keep my stomach under control.

"Is that what you wanted to know?" he said.

I nodded, still struggling to keep from throwing up. I had his nickname - Swizzle Stick Golgoran. No, that wasn't quite right. Swizzle Stick a Go Go. Yes, that was better.

"Those were the days," he said, sighing. "Things were much simpler then."

Then he looked at me, his face sharpening back into its worry lines.

"Enough reminiscing. Give me the Piece of Home."

I knew this was where we were headed. I'd known since the

moment I'd felt my cells coming apart. The thing is, I didn't know what I was going to do about it. Stupidly, I'd thought I'd be protected. I'd never planned for what would happen if the Enemy got me.

"I don't have it," I said. My hands started sweating.

"Of course you do," he said in a bored tone. "It's in a pouch around your neck hidden under your sweater."

What? How could he know?

I jumped up from my chair, my mind scrambling for my next move.

"You know what the Piece of Home can do?"

I nodded.

"Go on. Tell me."

"It allows you, I mean Satan, to re-fight the battle for heaven."

"Don't let Him hear you call him that. He prefers Abaddon."

Yeah. Whatever. We all knew who he was – Evil Incarnate.

"Is that all they told you?" He stared at me so intently that I took another step back.

"Yes," I said, my voice squeaking out the word.

He held my eyes, as though staring into my soul. Finally, he nodded.

"Give it to me." He held out his hand.

"I'm the only one that can handle it," I said, moving behind the chair. I hoped that was true. I knew the Descendants couldn't touch it without getting scorched, but maybe the Enemy was a different story.

"I've heard that but I don't believe it. Hand it over."

I'd like to say that I yelled "no" and went down fighting to the death to protect the Piece of Home. But something about Golgoran terrified me down to my bones. I didn't want to die.

I slowly lifted the cord over my neck, tipped the pouch over, and watched the glowing crystal slide into the palm of my hand.

Golgoran's eyes gleamed. Then he held out his hand and snapped his fingers.

"Put it right here Ariel," he said.

I plodded over to the desk. So much for being a hero. Feeling like a complete loser, I dropped the Piece of Home into his hand.

"Aargh!" Golgoran sprang up from his chair, the smell of burning flesh filling the room as the crystal fell to the floor. Tabitha let out a yip and ran under the desk. Golgoran stared at his hand, now marked with an angry blistered imprint of the crystal.

Golgoran opened a drawer in his desk and pulled out a stack of monogrammed handkerchiefs. Folding them in half until he had a big wad of cloth, he stooped and picked up the crystal.

"Ouch!" He dropped the crystal and his homemade potholder, which now had a black hole burned through the center.

He took a step back and studied the crystal, walking around it as though circling a hungry crocodile.

"Pick it up," he said, pointing at me.

I stooped and grabbed the crystal. It felt cool in my hand, just like it always did.

"Put it in the pouch and hand it to me," he said.

I slid the stone back into the pouch and held it out. He hesitated a moment and then reached for it. At the last minute, he extended his forefinger and touched the pouch.

"Ow," Golgoran spat out as I heard a sizzle and he jerked his finger away, which now sported a fat red blister.

"What have you done to it? Who are you?" he said in a dangerous voice, taking a step toward me.

"Me?" I said scuttling backward. "I haven't done anything. I don't know how to do anything. If I knew why no one can touch it but me I'd tell you. I don't even want it. I wish someone else *could* touch it. I'm the last person in the world who should have it. I'm a nobody."

I was babbling. All I could think of was my brain being turned into stew with a stir stick.

"Finally, something we can agree on," Golgoran said, eying me.

He paused, appearing to be in deep thought. I hoped it wasn't about what size of a bucket he'd need to drain my soupy brain into.

"And the same thing happens if the Descendants try to touch it? They get burned?" he said.

I nodded.

He walked over to his desk and pushed in the nose of one of the urchins on the corner.

"Yes, Master Golgoran," I heard a disjointed voice say.

"Send Aaron in here. Right now."

I hadn't thought I could get any more terrified, but I'd been wrong. If I'd been at Def Con 1 before, I was now at Def Con Zero – total meltdown. "Aaron" could only mean Michael's brother, the sadist whose picture was encased lovingly in Rosamund's locket.

I put the pouch holding the Piece of Home back around my neck almost without thinking and stumbled back over to the chair. I sank into it, putting my head between my knees, trying to regulate my breathing. Where were the Descendants? Why hadn't someone come to find me? How did Golgoran's men take me in the first place? And why was I the one stuck with this thing?

My head swam. I just wanted to go home to Dallas and pretend I'd never heard of Montana State or the Piece of Home.

The door swung open and I couldn't help but look up. A man just as gorgeous as Michael walked in the door. Same blue eyes, same dark hair, but more sharply defined features. He barely looked at me.

"It turns out that the reports were correct. No one can hold the thing except Ariel," Golgoran said. "All that planning, and we're not much closer than we were."

"So what do you want me to do about it?" Aaron said. He dropped into the chair opposite mine, stretching his legs out in front of him.

"I want you to fix it," Golgoran said, his tone menacing.

"This was your operation," Aaron said, scratching his ear. "Why should I help you? I owe you nothing. In fact, I'd say you're the one that owes me."

Golgoran glared at Aaron. Some unspoken communication passed between the two of them. Whatever it was, it wasn't pleasant.

"Okay, let's talk this through." Golgoran sat in the chair behind his desk, smoothed his tie and adjusted his pant cuffs over his boots.

"I'm listening," Aaron said, a smile playing at the edges of his mouth.

Golgoran cleared his throat. "If you'll help me, I'll give you the credit."

Aaron shook his head. "Your endorsement doesn't mean as much as it used to."

"That's just temporary. You know me. I'll get back on top."

"I'm not willing to gamble on that," Aaron said, leaning back in his chair.

"How about access to my apartment in Monte Carlo whenever you want? The women there are exquisite, I've got hundred-year-old bottles of wine in the cellar and a Bugatti to drive. It's magnificent."

"No."

"Okay, if you don't like Monte Carlo what about Paris? Or London? Or Budapest? Name it – I've got places and connections everywhere." Golgoran leaned his elbows onto the desk as he talked.

Aaron shook his head.

Golgoran sat back, glaring at Aaron. If his eyes could have thrown lightening bolts, Aaron would have burst into flame. I cringed back in my chair as though I might get caught in the crossfire.

Aaron yawned.

"What do you want?" Golgoran said, his voice cracking.

My mouth dropped open. Golgoran – pleading? It didn't compute. It was like watching Hercules beg.

"Turn the whole thing over to me," Aaron said, sitting up straight, his voice crisp. "Send out a memo to everyone telling them this is now my operation. Give me your resources, and tell your men they answer to me. And then you stay out of it. Don't question any of my decisions. Don't get in my way."

"That's ridiculous." Golgoran said.

"No problem," Aaron said, shrugging. "I don't want to do it anyway." He got to his feet. "Just out of curiosity, what's your plan?"

"I'm working on it," Golgoran said, sounding defensive. "At the very least, we could keep her here until we figure out how to handle the Piece of Home without spontaneously combusting."

"No," Aaron said, shaking his head. "If we do that they'll probably send some of their best to get her back, which means we'll lose a lot of personnel. Abaddon's already irritated at you over Frankie. You act like we have an infinite number of resources. If you cause the extinction of a number of our men, the least he'll do to you is bust you back down to minion rank, and it's very possible that he'll just exterminate you."

"I know, I know." Golgoran mopped his brow and sat in silence for a minute.

"Okay," he finally said. "We could just dispose of her, cut her hand off and duct tape the Piece of Home to it."

I gasped, tucking my hands under my thighs.

"Are you crazy?" Aaron said, staring at Golgoran.

Startled, I looked over at Aaron. Did he really care whether I got my hand cut off?

"You're clearly not yourself," Aaron said. "All the more reason why I should take over."

"Just hold on a minute," Golgoran said, twisting the ring on his pinkie. "Cutting her hand off might be the answer."

"How do you know it would work in a lifeless hand? How do you know it wouldn't burn the duct tape off? If it didn't work, then she'd be dead and we'd be totally out of options."

I guess Aaron wasn't squeamish about cutting my hand off after all. He just wasn't sure it would work.

Golgoran paced behind his desk, which was now totally alive, every single unspeakable being in motion, tearing and ripping at each other. Finally, he stopped and sank into his chair.

"Okay," he said.

"Okay, what?" Aaron said.

"Okay, I'll turn the whole thing over to you."

"And?"

"And you'll have full use of all my resources and no interference."

"All right then," Aaron said.

"So, what's your big idea?" Golgoran said.

"I'm not saying a word until you notify your people that I am now in charge of this operation."

"Where's the trust, Aaron?" Golgoran said, trying on a smile, but it slid off his face when Aaron's stony look didn't change.

"Okay, okay." Golgoran pressed the nose on the imp again.

"Yes," said a female voice.

"Come in and take a memo," he said.

A gorgeous young woman entered the room, her hips undulating provocatively beneath her skin-tight dress. Her hair glowed with a blue-black sheen, and her skin was so smooth it didn't seem to have a single pore, but the whole effect was ruined by the vapid look on her face. She carried a pencil and pad, and perched on the edge of Golgoran's desk.

"Ready, sir," she said.

Golgoran cleared his throat.

"To all Minions, Thugs and Henchmen in Quadrant 4, Northern Hemisphere. Operation Ariel is hereby and henceforth transferred to Aaron the Black. For matters related to that operation and solely to that operation...."

He stopped and gave Aaron a hard look and then continued.

"You are hereby instructed to follow his instructions and orders." He looked at the secretary. "Put my standard signature on that and send it out to everyone on the encrypted channel."

"Yes, sir," she said and slid off the desk.

"Not good enough," Aaron said.

The secretary stopped in mid-stride.

"Not good enough for what?" Golgoran said, looking startled.

"Don't pretend you don't know any better." Aaron crossed his arms. "I could walk out this door and ten seconds later you could rescind that order. Or if you don't like what I'm doing, you could send out a counter-instruction telling your men not to do that particular aspect. I want total control. Permanently. The order needs to say that it is non-rescindable."

"No," said Golgoran. "No way."

"Well then, good luck," Aaron said and strode toward the door. "I wouldn't want to be you when your little hand experiment doesn't work, or whatever else you dream up. You've just about used up all your goodwill."

"Hold on a second," Golgoran said. "We can work this out."

"No, we can't," Aaron said, turning to face him. "I don't know why you're fighting this so hard anyway. If it all goes south, I'll be the one to get the blame, not you."

"There's where you're wrong," Golgoran said. "I'll get the blame because I'm the one who gave you the job."

"Then it looks like you're in a no-win situation." Aaron grinned.

Golgoran glared at Aaron, and then his face sharpened.

"Just why do you want this operation so much anyway?" he said, his eyes narrowing. "We all know you're itching to get my job. If you think I'm going to fail, why not stand back and let it happen? Watching me fail seems like the better play."

Aaron remained silent.

"No," Golgoran said, slowly. "My intuition tells me I better hang onto this little operation myself."

"And that would be the same intuition that has you barricaded in your office with, what is that, a therapy dog?" Aaron pointed at the Yorkie cowering under the desk. "The rumors are true – you are losing it."

"Vivienne," Golgoran said, jerking his head at the secretary, "you may leave now. And burn that memo when you get to your desk."

"Yes sir," she said, and minced out of the room.

"And the hits just keep on coming," Aaron said, snorting. "Let's see, so far you've been tied in knots by a mere girl. You let her kill Achimalech, your best mole inside the Exiles and then she beat you to finding the Piece of Home first. It's taken you a month to pick her up but during that time you made zero preparation for what to do about taking possession of the Piece of Home even though your spies told you it burned everyone but her. I guess you've been the boss for so long that you started to believe your own press. It must have been a shock when even you, the mighty Golgoran, couldn't touch the Piece of Home without burning your hand off." He stared pointedly at Golgoran's right hand which still sported a red stripe, although it looked much better than it had just moments ago.

"Get out," Golgoran yelled.

"Gladly," Aaron said. "And you're right. I am going to love seeing you go down." He turned and sauntered out the door.

Golgoran marched over and bent to glare at me eyeball to eyeball. A vein throbbed in his forehead. I shrank back in my chair.

"I'm going to figure out how to take the Piece of Home from you, and then I'm going to kill you. Personally," he said, giving me a nasty smile that would have made Attila the Hun turn and run. "And I'm going to enjoy it more than anything I've done in a thousand years."

"Vivienne," he yelled, straightening.

Vivienne ran back into the room, wobbling on her high heels. I guess speed and grace don't go together when you're wearing six inch stilettos. At least this time she had a bit of animation on her face.

"Get the boys and tell them to put this girl in the holding area."

"Yes sir," she said, and dashed back out the door.

Seconds later, Raspy and Squeaky edged into the room.

"You want that we should take her outta here, boss?" Raspy said.

"Didn't Vivienne tell you to take her to the holding area?" Golgoran snapped.

"Well, yeah. We was just making sure..."

"So then do it, you imbeciles."

Raspy's face flushed, and he nodded to Squeaky. They grabbed my arms and frog- marched me toward the door.

"I'll see you soon, Ariel," Golgoran said. "Count on it."

That's what I was afraid of.

CHAPTER THIRTEEN

SOOTERKIN: A SWEETHEART OR MISTRESS

Sixteen Years Ago: Murder Trial, Evening of the Third Day

"Don't even think about it." Irene Spicklemeyer glared at the approaching guard.

"It's standard procedure, ma'am," the guard said, the smirk on his face belying his dispassionate tone.

"No it is not. I've been through the metal detector and relinquished all my bobby pins." Mrs. Spicklemeyer gestured to her hair which, released from her usual severe bun, now cascaded down her back in loose waves. "I made sure to wear clothes with buttons, rubber soled shoes, and my handbag has been confiscated."

The guard shrugged. "Ma'am, I don't make the rules. I just follow them."

"If you think you're going to pat me down, you've got another think coming," she said, her voice steely.

He advanced another step and she took one back.

"Wait. I know you from somewhere." Her eyes narrowed.

"We've never met, ma'am. Now I'd appreciate it if you'd cooperate. Otherwise – "

"Otherwise what?"

"I can promise you, ma'am, you don't want to find out," he said, but the smirk on his face widened into a nasty grin.

"That's it." She snapped her fingers. "Little Billy Weston."

The smile vanished and his face reddened.

"Yes. It was all that ma'aming and the smirk." Now she was the one with a smirk on her face. "I remember you."

"Ma'- I mean Mrs. Spicklemeyer, this will only take a second and then you can – "

"You know that I work for Lucian Castlewhite, right?" Billy's face turned from red to ash white. "Do your employers know about your past, Billy?"

"My name is not Billy. It's Will."

"You didn't answer my question. Do they know about your past, young man?"

"I don't know what you're talking about."

"Prevarication is not an attractive quality, Will." Mrs. Spicklemeyer's voice was as pedantic as that of an Old West school marm.

"Prevari - what?"

"Prevarication – it means to perpetuate or employ a canard."

Will's brow furrowed.

"A canard is a lie, Will. You don't want to go through life lying. We both know what you did. My question is, does your employer here at the jail know about it?"

"That record was sealed." Will's face flushed red.

"I imagine that doesn't make much difference to your employer.

In the space on your application where it asked whether you'd ever been arrested, I'm guessing you put 'no'".

Will said nothing.

"And you certainly didn't tell them you'd actually been convicted of – "

"You can go on through now," Will said, going to the wide door and pulling it open.

"Thank you Will," Mrs. Spicklemeyer said, smiling.

One of the few perks of working for a defense lawyer was knowledge of the peccadillos, big and small, of one's neighbors. Will had loved playing practical jokes, but had gone a bit too far when, years ago, he'd applied super glue to all the seats at the Council table immediately before a big meeting. Madame Chairperson had not been pleased when the back of her new velvet robe had stayed behind when she'd risen at the conclusion of the meeting. Fortunately, she had pants on underneath.

Other members of the Council had not been so fortunate.

Under severe political pressure, the prosecutor had thrown the book at Will, jacking up what should have been a simple misdemeanor, if that, to a class C felony – aggravated criminal mischief - claiming that the property damage to the chairs from the superglue provided the basis for the enhanced charge. Lucian had successfully argued that the only aggravation at play was one prominent Council member's pique at having those present learn that he didn't wear underwear and that his cottage cheese backside revealed a fact everyone already knew – that he didn't exercise or follow a sensible diet.

The Court found Will guilty of simple mischief and he was ordered to serve one year of probation, pay for the damage to the chairs and purchase Madame Chairperson a new robe. Since he'd been a youngster, the record had been sealed once he successfully completed his probation.

Mrs. Spicklemeyer's smile faded as she approached the

squishy-looking door at the end of the hall. Another guard swung it open, and she entered the room.

The Defendant leapt to his feet when he saw her, rounding the rectangular table where he'd been sitting to clasp her in a bear hug.

He pulled back, his hands burying in her hair, his forehead resting on hers.

"No bun today, Irene?" he said, his voice teasing.

"Bobby pins," she said, blushing. She loved it when he ran his fingers through her hair.

"No touching," the guard said.

The Defendant gave her a final squeeze, and then returned to his seat. Mrs. Spicklemeyer perched in the metal chair across from him.

"Please leave the room," Mrs. Spicklemeyer said in a no-nonsense voice, glaring at the guard.

"That is not part of the protocol," he said.

"I'm a member of the Defendant's legal team. Our conversations are privileged. Do you want me to advise the Court that you're depriving the Defendant of the ability to freely converse with his counsel?"

"But you're his girlfriend and – "

"One can occupy two distinct categories – I can be both a girlfriend and a paralegal. Aren't you aware of the *Standish v. Bank of the Rockies* case in which the Court of Appeals decided that very issue?"

The guard looked uncomfortable but didn't move.

"Fine." Mrs. Spicklemeyer sighed, and then rose from the table. "I'll draft an emergency motion, drag the judge away from his dinner, and tell him that his steak has grown cold because the prison doesn't care to follow the law. He'll love that."

The guard stared at Mrs. Spicklemeyer. She stared back.

"Okay," he said. "But I'm going to be checking on you."

He backed out of the room and closed the door.

"*Standish v. Bank of the Rockies*?" The Defendant's eyes twinkled.

"Well, you know that's the law, even if I don't have an exact case cite. And *Standish v. Bank of the Rockies* sounds so much better than *Smith v. Jones*."

He laughed. "It's so good to see you, Irene. I've missed you."

"I've missed you too, darling. So much." Eyes glistening with tears, she sank back into her chair. After a moment, she cleared her throat.

"So how are the pugs? Has Roscoe accepted Waldo yet?" the Defendant said.

Just before the Defendant had been arrested, Mrs. Spicklemeyer had gotten a new pug puppy to keep her seven year old pug, Roscoe, company. Roscoe hadn't appreciated the gift, but Waldo hadn't seemed to notice, epitomizing the term 'puppy love' in his slavish adoration of Roscoe.

"He's tolerating him. It's hard not to warm up to being worshipped."

A moment passed while the two just sat, fingers touching across the table. Finally, Mrs. Spicklemeyer straightened.

"Lucian asked me to come and talk to you," she began.

"So that's why you're here," the Defendant said. His tone was mild but his eyes hardened a millimeter.

"Oh sweetheart, you know I'd come anyway. It's about Rachel."

"It's always about Rachel." The Defendant pulled his fingers away from hers. "I'm sick of talking about Rachel. Can't we just talk about normal things and forget about the nightmare for just a few minutes?"

Mrs. Spicklemeyer shifted in her chair.

"I'd love to, darling, but this is important. Please."

"All right," the Defendant said, his shoulders slumping. "What is it? Surely you don't believe that I had any romantic interest in that girl?"

"Of course not," she said. "I know you'd have nothing to do with that silly twit."

She meant it. She'd known the Defendant for years, even back before his wife died. Up until a year ago, she'd thought she knew almost everything about him. He liked to read four newspapers every morning – the New York Times, the Wall Street Journal, the Denver Post and the local paper. He took his coffee black, loved crossword puzzles, couldn't get enough of the game of baseball, and was satisfied with a wardrobe of one black suit, one navy suit, two pairs of khaki pants and an assortment of brightly colored golf shirts.

He played poker on Wednesday nights, went to the opera and tinkered in his basement with building model 16th century sailing ships. On Saturdays, he played golf, and on Sundays he worked in the garden.

When his wife had died, his grief had been dignified and contained. He talked a little less, but remained unfailingly polite. He had a veneer that was paradoxically warm but still kept one at a distance. Everyone felt comfortable in telling him anything, and most of the time they never realized that he shared little of his own personal feelings. Mrs. Spicklemeyer had liked and admired him, but thought he was a bit of a bore. She and the Defendant were cordial with each other, but despite all the years of their acquaintance, they'd never used each other's first names.

All that had changed one evening a year earlier. Mrs. Spicklemeyer's pug, Roscoe, had been bitten by a snake and she'd rushed him to the animal hospital. The Defendant had run into her there, having given a ride to a neighbor with a sick cat.

He'd taken one look at her in the waiting room – her red, swollen eyes, her runny nose, her hair straggling haphazardly from her usual neat bun – and folded her into his arms. Together, they waited for the doctor to give them the prognosis. He'd helped her take Roscoe home and had sat up with her through the night, watching Roscoe just as intently as she did.

Somehow, in the relief over Roscoe and in the magic of the late night hours, the veneer had dropped. The Defendant had confided in her his deepest secret – that he'd never really loved his wife, but had married her out of some misguided sense of obligation. Even though she wasn't the love of his life, they'd had a comfortable marriage, and he'd worked hard to make it so. He'd believed he'd successfully hidden his feelings from her all the way up until the day he discovered her body in their bedroom. She'd committed suicide. She'd left no note, leaving him to wonder what had been going on in her mind on that fateful morning, and the guilt of possibly having a hand in her death had twisted like a knife in his stomach ever since.

In return, Mrs. Spicklemeyer had told him about her one and only romance, a manipulating Lothario who'd flattered her, wooed her, and ultimately cleaned out every dime she had. Since then, she'd never dared to trust her instincts about any man and had lived as a single woman, steadily growing more and more set in her ways and developing the persona of a hardened spinster, the kind no one could ever imagine having had a childhood, much less a personal life.

By the time dawn broke, Roscoe was demanding treats, they were calling each other "Irene" and "Zach", and they'd shared their first kiss.

Six months later, he'd given her a beautiful blue sapphire engagement ring surrounded by diamonds and they'd set a wedding date. The relationship had caused a lot of speculation and amusement in the Mountain. Neither were seen as being particularly attractive, or even capable of having a searing hot romance, and since they were both uber-dignified in public, no one had a clue that they were the kind of couple who gave each other scented oil massages, enjoyed romantic candle-lit evenings, and whispered pet names to each other too embarrassing to put into print.

The Defendant had changed the trajectory of Irene Spicklemeyer's life, and she felt as beautiful, loved and cherished as Helen of Troy, the woman two countries were willing to fight over.

She had absolutely no doubt that the Defendant had been faithful to her.

"Lucian believes..." she hesitated, "we both believe that it's crucial to let the jury know about Rachel's constant disappearances. For all we know, she's not even dead, but has run off with some boy."

"No." The Defendant's face hardened into stone.

"But – "

"I said no. I won't allow it. And I don't want to talk about it anymore."

"Why? We can prove that she was gone almost every weekend, and that she was so secretive about it that no one knows where she went. She was probably sneaking off to spend time with some married man, and if anyone killed her, it was probably – "

"Guard," the Defendant said in a loud voice, standing so abruptly that his chair almost fell over.

"Honey – "

"Guard," the Defendant called again, and the door swung open. His eyes met Mrs. Spicklemeyer's. "I told you I don't want to talk about it."

"Please." Tears sprang to her eyes. "What's going on?"

He turned his face away and strode toward the guard. Just before he reached the door he turned back.

"Tell Lucian that if either you or he bring up this subject again, I will fire him and defend myself. Do you understand?"

He stared at her, waiting for an answer.

She looked back at him, unable to believe her ears.

"But – "

"Do you understand?" His voice echoed in the room, so loud that it hurt her ears.

Slowly she nodded.

"And don't come see me again." He stared off somewhere past her left shoulder. "I'm taking you off of my visitor's list."

He turned and walked out the door.

CHAPTER FOURTEEN

Befuddle:
To confuse, perplex

"Did you check her for weapons?" Squeaky asked after the door had closed behind us.

"No, I thought you did." Raspy jerked to a stop. He patted me down as gingerly as though he were checking a suicide bomber with a dead man switch. "She's clean."

My escorts drug me along, practically running, through the hallways. They acted like I had ebola or something, and the quicker they got rid of me, the less chance they'd have of getting infected.

I craned my head around, taking in the scene as we rushed from hallway to hallway. While the Descendants' headquarters glowed with a honey-colored light, The Enemy's Headquarters were lit with an electric, greenish glow, like being inside a computer screen.

The floors were black slate, and video screens hung on some of the walls, sound muted, showing everything from CNN to The

Kardashians to Al Jazeera to stations in languages I couldn't understand. My head swiveled as we passed a room filled with nerdy looking types seated behind computer screens, all facing a huge screen on the far wall showing areas of green, yellow and red pulsating on a flattened depiction of the globe, with more televisions populating the other walls. It looked like some kind of a situation room. The whole place had a military vibe.

At the end of the hall, a door opened into a stairwell. The men hustled me down two flights of stairs which ended in front of a steel door. Squeaky entered a code on the keypad next to it, and the door swung open with a hiss.

Cold air blew into my face, briefly lifting the strands of my hair. The door shut behind us, sounding exactly like a refrigerator door. They pushed me through to another hall with plain walls until we reached a squishy looking door with another electronic keypad by its frame. Raspy entered a code, opened the door, and then shoved me in. The door slammed behind me. My breath fogged in front of my face.

I looked around. The room looked like the kind of accommodation reserved for someone on death row. It felt cramped, even to someone my size. A lidless toilet sat in the corner, and a cot took up the whole wall across from it. The only light came from a glow somewhere in the ceiling which was a good ten feet over my head.

I shivered, feeling the room's chill seep through my coat. Were they trying to save money by not heating their prison?

That's when I caught the faint whiff of something rotten, that sick, decaying smell that told me someone had died in here. Maybe that's why they kept the room refrigerated – to dampen the smell. But I didn't think the Enemy would be overly concerned with its prisoners' comfort. Maybe it was the cold that was keeping the smell alive, as though it had taken months, or even years, for the odor to mellow from an unbearable reek to an unpleasant undertone.

I paced the perimeter of the room looking for an escape. I

pounded on the spongy walls which did nothing but make my hands ache. Shivering, I sank to the floor.

Who knows how long it would take before Michael even knew I was gone? If Rosamund was in on it, she wouldn't even tell anyone I was gone until she absolutely had to. She could even say I was sick for a couple of days and that's why I wasn't leaving the dorm just to buy the Enemy more time.

Tears sprang to my eyes. I could be dead before anyone came looking for me.

And the Piece of Home? If the Enemy got it, the whole world would be in jeopardy. I tried to focus on that instead of just on my own limited future, but I had a hard time doing it. I know my life is not as important as the fate of the world – at least in theory – but my logical side was having a hard time convincing my emotional side of that fact.

Maybe if the battle for heaven were re-fought, the Enemy would lose. On the other hand, they seemed awfully confident that they had the numbers to win.

For the first time in my life, I couldn't find a rosy interpretation of what was happening. The glass was, in fact, half empty. The cloud had no silver lining. The lemons were too rotten to make lemonade. The light at the end of the tunnel was a bullet train at full speed. The rose-colored glasses fell to the floor and shattered.

Minutes passed. Tears dripped. Nothing changed.

"Well bless your heart."

I started, hearing Swisbo's voice just as clearly as though she'd been standing over me. If she blessed your heart, then you'd just received one of her worst insults. Like our neighbor Mr. Plemons "means well, but bless his heart he wouldn't know it was raining unless someone handed him an umbrella" or my friend Katie "is a lovely girl, but bless her heart how does her mother let her leave the house in that outfit?"

Swisbo took it one step further. Whenever I balked at doing

something she thought was good for me, she'd smack me with a bless-your-heart. Don't want to take that extra credit course? "Well, bless your heart you'll probably do just fine in community college until you can get into a four year school." Or when I wanted to extend my curfew on weeknights it was "bless your heart, maybe you're right. When you're stuck waitressing at Bud's Diner because you slept through class, at least you'll have these wonderful years to look back on."

She's a bit sarcastic.

Over time, all she'd have to do is look at me and say "bless your heart". Then I'd know I was in trouble, usually for not doing something she thought I should be doing – like volunteering at the senior center or taking an extra credit class.

Her voice in my brain forced me to my feet. Maybe there was some way out of this room.

I scanned the room, looking for anything that showed some weakness in the walls or the door. But then something caught my eye on the far wall. Scratches.

I scurried over and knelt in front of it, peering at the lines. Someone had pressed a makeshift pen deep into the wall, hard enough to leave a permanent indentation. I squinted at the characters, reading and re-reading them.

Huh.

C(s): 1274 - -1544F→C(g)
C(s): 10 GPa + 8540.33→C(l)
EC = 12992-1598 and GPa > 10

The "7" had a dash through the middle, like my Calculus professor used to distinguish between a "1" and a "7".

Somebody had been calculating something. That's all I could make of the numbers, although C could be carbon.

I felt my skin prickle, as though someone were watching me.

I whirled, looking around the room for hidden cameras, but saw nothing. Maybe the Enemy didn't even need cameras. They could probably just see right through the walls.

I turned back to the numbers, tracing them with my fingers. They made no sense.

And then I heard a click and felt a rush of air. A warm hand covered my eyes, and a strong arm encircled my waist, holding me in place.

"Don't say a word," a synthetic voice whispered in my ear. "I'm here to help you."

I started shaking.

"Shh. Shh. It's okay. I'm going to get you out of here. But you have to remember one thing."

He or she or it pulled me toward the cell door, which was open, and out into the hallway.

"Wh – Who are you," I said.

"A friend. That's not important now. What you have to remember is that you can't trust anyone."

The voice sounded so eerie, like one of those electronic gadgets kidnappers used to disguise their voices.

I shook even harder.

"Did you hear me Ariel?"

I nodded.

"Say it," the voice said.

"I can't trust anyone," I repeated.

"Right. Golgoran has moles and spies everywhere. I don't even know who all of them are because he keeps that information secret. And someone who isn't a mole may be confiding in someone who is. So, that means you can't trust anyone."

"Even Michael?" The words left my mouth before I even knew I was going to say them.

"Yes, even Michael."

I couldn't breathe. Dread seeped down my spine.

"Are you saying that he actually is a mole or are you saying that he could be talking to a mole without knowing it?"

I felt the familiar loosening of my cells and a whoosh of air.

"Good luck," the voice whispered and then whoever was holding me let go.

I spun around.

No one was there. I was back in the laundry room.

I looked down at my watch. Two hours had passed. My laundry was clean, dry, and neatly folded in the laundry basket with the log-book and my phone resting on top.

The locket which I'd left lying on the table was gone.

CHAPTER FIFTEEN

Benedict Arnold: A traitor

The minute I calmed down enough to talk, I grabbed my phone and started to hit speed dial for Michael. Then I stopped.

What to do? I needed help. I couldn't protect myself alone, and somehow the Enemy had taken me even though supposedly no one could get through my protection. Wouldn't the Enemy just come right back and get me?

Who else could I trust, particularly after what had just happened? There was always Barnaby, but I wasn't sure what he could do to help me. And Lucian...

Crap. I'd forgotten to call Lucian. I looked down at my phone and saw that I had twelve missed calls and four texts, all from Lucian. I entered the last number I had for him, waited through several clicks, and then heard a ringing sound on the other end.

Lucian is paranoid about everyone. Even though he's a Descendant himself, he trusts them only marginally more than the Enemy. I'm sure any phone call gets bounced off satellites all over the world before it hits his cell, and he's lamented the demise of the landline as the biggest step forward for spies everywhere since the invention of disappearing ink.

Most of the time, I think his precautions are a little ridiculous, the equivalent of wearing a foil hat to prevent a brain wipe by virulent gamma rays that don't exist except in the mind of the wearer.

"Ariel?" Lucian sounded anxious. "Are you all right?"

"Yes," I said. "Just barely."

"What happened?"

I hesitated, and then told him, leaving nothing out. If you can't trust your lawyer, who can you trust? Besides, as far as I could tell, he'd always been careful to stay outside of the Descendants' camp.

"Oh no. Where are you?"

"I'm still in the laundry room. I don't know where to go." My voice rose, my words tumbling over one another. "Rosamund might be in my room, and if she's with them she'll know I've escaped, and I'm afraid to call Michael, not that I think he's with the Enemy but he did trust Rosamund so what does that say about his judgment and..." I stopped, willing myself not to burst into tears.

"Oh Ariel. I'm so sorry."

I gulped in some air. "It's not your fault."

"Yes it is." He sounded angry. "I knew something was wrong but I was too far away to get to you. If I could transport I could have come back and gotten you away before anything happened."

"It's okay." I didn't blame Lucian for his transport phobia. Theoretically, he could do it but couldn't bring himself to try. I didn't blame him. I hated transporting too. "I'm the one who didn't look at my phone. But how did you know something was wrong?"

"Just a minute, Ariel. Do we turn left here?" he said, his voice a bit muffled.

"Yes," I heard a female voice say.

"Are you driving?" I said.

"Yes, and Mrs. Spicklemeyer is with me."

I hoped they weren't too far away. Here's the thing about my lawyer – he's smart, can keep a secret, and isn't afraid to take on anybody, even Abaddon. But not only is he afraid to transport, he drives like someone who's only been behind the wheel once or twice. He refuses to drive even a smidge over the speed limit, and white-knuckles the steering wheel like he's maneuvering a fission bomb that could blow up without warning.

"I discovered that the surveillance sector where you are was put on auto repeat. I started back immediately."

"Huh?"

"That means that the security system the Descendants use to help keep you safe registered data from a different time period and played it as though it were happening live."

"So..." I still wasn't sure what he meant.

"When the Enemy took you, there was no thermal, audio, visual or particle evidence that you were gone. It's like disabling the system in a very sophisticated way. They actually used the data from the same day and time last week, so it would look to the casual observer like everything was normal. Anyone watching would see you doing what you always do on Fridays."

"Wow," I said, trying to digest the information that I'd had such a system watching over me, much less that it had been disabled. Did that mean that the army of Descendants Michael had assured me repeatedly were watching over me were really just watching a computer screen?

"But how did you know? And why didn't anyone else see the problem?" What I really meant was why the heck didn't Michael know about it.

"I have electronic trip wires set up all over the place. I know when someone is fiddling with the system. I'm guessing that it never occurred to the Descendants that the system could be gamed."

My stomach knotted as I digested Lucian's information. "Who could do something like that?"

"I don't know." Lucian sighed. "This is a sophisticated operation. It takes more than one person to monitor that data because it has so much information. It literally tracks the atoms of everything and everyone you come into contact with. That's the only way you can monitor the movements of the Enemy. And it would take a team of people to copy all that data from the previous week, pause the live data in just your sector, and load the copied data without crashing the system. And the access codes involved..." his voice trailed off.

"I'm afraid your rescuer was right," he continued, his voice serious. "You can't trust anyone. The Enemy's operation inside the Descendants' headquarters is bigger than I would have ever imagined."

"What do I do? How do I keep from getting taken again? Where should I go?" I looked around the laundry room, which was still strangely empty. Lucian was silent.

"Lucian?"

"Hold on a moment," he said, and then his voice took on that distorted quality, as though he were covering the phone. "Mrs. Spicklemeyer? Could you check the security grids again on your laptop?"

I heard something that sounded like an electronic beep in the background and then keys tapping.

"Good news. They've gone back to the real surveillance data. I bet they were only able to substitute it for a limited period of time. You should be safe for the moment."

"Really?" I gulped.

"Yes. They may try again, but if the system is tampered with I'll know it, and will call you immediately. It should take them at least another day to get the data loaded up to try again, and if the only day they copied was the data that matches your schedule for today, they may have to wait another week."

"Golgoran did make some comment to Aaron about having done a lot of planning only to have it come to nothing because they couldn't touch the Piece of Home."

"He's right. I can't begin to tell you how complicated it is to disable the system like they did. To put the system on auto-repeat, you have to separately upload every function and measurement that the security system does, which is incredibly time-consuming. It was a brilliant idea and well executed. We're lucky you had a rescuer."

I swallowed. The thought of all that brain power and animus devoted to kidnapping me made me woozy. I'd never been the object of this much attention, much less malevolent attention.

I may be naïve but I'm not stupid. Even I understood that no matter what assurances Michael gave me, my safety had become TMP – totally my problem.

"What's your schedule this weekend? Where can I find you?" Lucian said.

"You know what this weekend is, Lucian," I heard Mrs. Spicklemeyer say. "It's Parents' Weekend. Her parents are coming today and will be here all weekend."

"Oh, yes, that's right," Lucian said. "Wonderful. The Enemy won't try anything with them around. That would create too much attention if you disappeared right under their noses. Where are they staying?"

"They rented a house. Swis- I mean Mom didn't like the hotel options."

"I think you should ask to stay with them," he said. "Every minute you can spend with them is a minute when the Enemy won't dare snatch you."

"Okay," I said, surprised by my own instant willingness. I loved my parents, but I'd spent my whole high school senior year chafing to get away. Now, after all that had happened, the thought of spending time with prickly Swisbo felt like the equivalent of a fluffy comforter, a cup of chicken soup, and a foot warmer all rolled into one.

"I'll call you if the security system gets tinkered with in any way, so leave your phone on," he said.

"Don't worry," I said. No way was I turning it off.

"In the meantime, I'm going to see what I can do about getting you some reliable protection."

"Don't worry, sweetie," Mrs. Spicklemeyer said. "We're on it."

Instead of reassuring me, Mrs. Spicklemeyer's words brought my pulse rate back up a titch. She never says words like "sweetie" or "honey", at least to me. Was that a good sign or a bad sign?

"Ariel?" Lucian said.

"Yes?"

"I said, I'm sure I can find someone to help look out for you. Don't worry."

"Oh, yes," I said. "Thanks."

We exchanged goodbyes and I gathered my laundry basket and made my way back to my room.

My steps slowed as I neared the door.

What would I say to Rosamund? I was almost positive she'd been in on the whole kidnapping plot. Should I confront her?

No. I'm pretty sure she could kick my butt, and, if she's desperate, no telling what she might do.

Should I act like nothing had happened?

Impossible, and she'd know better.

Maybe I shouldn't go back to my room.

Good idea.

I stopped at the end of the hall and pulled out my phone again.

"Who loves ya baby!" Barnaby's voice crashed through the phone. I held it away from my ear.

"Hey Barnaby."

"I need to talk to Michael."

"Aw, Ariel. I told you, no can do, sugar pop," he said. "It's crazy busy around here. It's big poobah central at HQ. Michael's been in meetings all day."

"I have to see him, Barnaby. It's important."

"I know, I know. You're going to die if you don't see him, right?"

"Right." Wow. Barnaby was more perceptive than I thought.

"You've got it bad." He chuckled. "You're jonesing for a Michael fix, huh. I feel ya but it's not possible. He'll see you at dinner with your parents."

"Barnaby! I mean it – I have to..." I heard noises in the background.

"Whoops –gotta go," he said. "Talk to ya later babe." The line went dead.

I hit redial. No answer. Crap.

I pressed my hands to my temples, trying to contain the throbbing in my head. No matter what the electric-voiced stranger had said, I just couldn't believe Michael was one of the bad guys. After the whole Achimalech fiasco, though, I could definitely believe that other traitors had infiltrated the Descendants' Headquarters. And no matter what my rescuer had said, I had to trust someone, right?

I mentally composed my "safe" list. Michael, Barnaby, Lucian and Mrs. Spicklemeyer. And Daniel and Cyrus. Good enough.

Now, what to do about Rosamund. There was really only one thing I could do. I'd tell her what happened, yell at her for not protecting me, and in general act like I have zero suspicion that she's with the Enemy. Time to test my acting skills.

I straightened, sucked in a deep breath, eased the door open, and stepped in.

The room was pin neat for the first time since Rosamund had moved in. All her things were gone. No clothes, no shoes, no jewelry, no magazines. It was as if she'd never been there.

She'd definitely been in on it.

CHAPTER SIXTEEN

FOURBERIE: DECEIT, TRICKERY, GUILE

Sixteen Years Ago: Murder Trial, Day 5

Lucian had known something dark and deadly had been at play since the beginning. Probably something political, although he guessed he'd never know. But over the past week he'd made the mistake of daring to hope.

"Stupid, stupid man," he thought. It was all he could do now to remain upright after the gut punch he's just received. The judge's chambers felt dark and claustrophobic, the lighting as dim as his client's prospects.

"Your Honor, we had no notice of this evidence. It begs credulity to believe that the prosecution just now found it. Its origins are highly suspect. There is nothing to link it with my client other than the location in which it was found, which had already been searched countless times by the investigators. Further, the prosecution has already rested their case, we are about to rest ours, and allowing this evidence in now would unduly prejudice the Defendant."

"I resent the implication that the evidence was planted, Your Honor," the prosecutor said, his aggrieved tone failing to match the smug look on his face. "We've never given up looking, thank goodness. As soon as it was found, I notified defense counsel. That's what I was obligated to do, and that's what I did. Furthermore, if the Defendant hadn't hidden it, we would have found it months ago. It would be unjust to allow the Defendant to profit from his own deception."

"How do we know the evidence wasn't planted?" Lucian said. "The Defendant has been in jail for six months. Anyone could have put it there. And how, by the way, did the prosecution suddenly happen upon this evidence?"

"That is a question I would like answered," said the judge, fixing the prosecutor with a stare.

"We received a tip." The prosecutor fidgeted with his tie.

"From who?" the judge said.

"We don't know. It came in anonymously."

"Then Judge, it has to be disallowed. It would be too prejudicial to allow it in when the timing and manner of discovery are so highly suspect." Lucian tried to keep his voice from revealing the panic rising in his throat.

"Your Honor, please," the prosecutor said, his voice silken. "It was found behind a wall in the Defendant's home, undoubtedly where he hid it months ago. The only fingerprints on it are his. The probative value far outweighs any prejudice."

"I agree," said the judge after a pause. "I'm letting it in with an instruction."

"But Your Honor..." Lucian jumped to his feet.

The judge raised his hands. "Now, now Mr. Castlewhite. You can bring up all the questions about the timing of the discovery and make what you can out of the anonymous phone tip. I'll give you a lot of leeway in your cross-examination. But the light sword found in your client's home is coming in."

CHAPTER SEVENTEEN

Descry:
To Detect, Perceive

Something was wrong.

Swisbo hadn't made one critical comment – not about my room, my hair or my clothes. Sure, I'd fluffed my hair, put on slacks instead of jeans and pulled on the girly sweater with tiny rosebuds she'd bought for me last Christmas (one she had to know I'd hate), but those acts were designed to stave off the initial salvo. Based on years of experience, I knew there would be a couple or twenty items that wouldn't pass muster with her and I'd braced myself for it.

But here we were, two hours into the visit, and she hadn't pelted me with a single rock-in-the-marshmallow comment. You know, ones where she says something like, "luckily you're so pretty that you manage to pull off these hideous hairstyles girls your age favor". Maybe my dad had persuaded her to cut me some slack on her visit to my first home away from home.

On the other hand, she hadn't said much about anything. After coming to my dorm and taking a brief tour of the campus, we'd gone to Ted's, the restaurant Lucian had recommended when I'd asked him where I should take my parents for dinner. Swisbo had yet to even look at the menu. She twisted her napkin in her lap, fidgeted with the silverware, and had excused herself from the table twice – once to go to the restroom and once to "stretch her legs", all of which went against her usual rigid table etiquette. Watching her, for the first time I saw fine lines radiating around her mouth and what looked like a permanent furrow on her brow.

"Are you feeling okay, honey?" my dad said, putting his hand on her arm.

"Yes," she said, but then looked down at her hand playing with the fork as though it belonged to someone else. She put it down and clasped both hands together on the table.

"So, Ariel," she said. "I thought your friend – Michael, is it? – was going to join us for dinner."

Yeah, I'd thought so too. He'd stood me up, texting some ridiculous excuse about work thirty minutes before he was supposed to meet us. I hadn't texted him back, not trusting my thumbs to stay civil.

I mean, it's not like he has some boss insisting on overtime. I got the message. I was ready to give him a message of my own next time I saw him.

He'd said he'd catch up with us sometime over the weekend. I wasn't going to hold my breath. I ping-ponged between hurt and anger, trying to keep the tiny seed of suspicion from growing into an impenetrable forest. Was Michael interested in me, or only in the crystal I held? Was I just a means to an end? I'd been kidnapped by the Enemy, rescued by Electric Voice, abandoned by my bodyguard, and I hadn't been able to reach Michael to tell him about it. And now he'd blown off meeting the parents.

He was flunking the boyfriend test big time.

"He had a lot of work to do," I said, knowing how pitiful that sounded even before Swisbo exchanged a meaningful look with my dad.

My phone dinged with a text. My mother glared at me.

"I'm only keeping it on in case...." I said, pausing as I read the message.

"Is Samantha with you?" It was from Todd.

"No," I texted back.

The phone dinged again.

"Ariel," my mother said. "You know my rules. You're being rude."

I nodded, and tried not to look back at the screen, a feat as difficult as not looking at the sun during a solar eclipse.

The waiter appeared. "Have we decided?"

"Honey," my dad said looking at Swisbo. "Do you know what you want?"

"I..."

Ding, ding, ding.

"Turn that thing off," she said, glaring at me.

I lifted the phone from my lap and saw the messages.

"She was supposed to meet me an hour ago."

"She's not in her room."

"She's not answering her phone."

I read Todd's messages, my stomach doing a mini-flip. Samantha could be scatter-brained and perpetually ran late for everything, but she never, ever let her phone out of her sight. She'd find a way to answer it even if she were in the middle of her own wedding.

"Isn't she with her parents?" I texted back.

"Ariel," Swisbo said with an edge to her voice. "I'm not going to ask again."

Really. What age did I have to be before I could set my own rules for phone use?

"It's important," I said, lifting my chin. "Samantha might be missing."

"I think we're going to need a little more time," my dad said, looking at the waiter, who scuttled away, looking grateful. I wasn't sure we'd ever see him again.

Ding. "Her parents went home."

I caught a movement out of the corner of my eye. Lucian and Mrs. Spicklemeyer were being seated three tables away. What were they doing here?

"Excuse me," I said to my parents. "I'll be right back. I think I see one of my, um, professors." I didn't know if my dad would recognize Lucian from all those years ago when he'd brought me to him to adopt, and I didn't know if I wanted to explain the coincidence of Lucian and I being acquainted. I hustled over to his table.

"Is everything okay?" I said, my heart pounding. "Has the grid – or whatever it is – gone down again?"

"No, no," he said, looking a little sheepish. "Everything's fine. I just thought I'd keep an eye on you. Besides, this is Mrs. Spicklemeyer's favorite restaurant." He must have seen the slight panic in my eyes. "I'm pretty sure your dad won't recognize me." His face dropped and he suddenly looked sad. "I've aged quite a bit since then. Right?" He looked over at Mrs. Spicklemeyer for confirmation. But she wasn't looking at him. She was staring at something behind me, her face ashen.

Lucian followed her gaze, his own face turning from pink to red to purple. I turned to look. They were staring at my parents. No, they were staring at Swisbo.

Mrs. Spicklemeyer jumped to her feet and rushed toward Swisbo, with Lucian following after her.

She blew to a stop inches from Swisbo, who stood up so fast that she knocked her chair over.

"You little....," Mrs. Spicklemeyer said in a whisper. And then again, louder. "You Jezebel. All this time. Do you know what you did to him?"

Swisbo scurried backward, stumbling into the lap of a diner

at the next table, a thirty-something year old man who gingerly steadied her as she popped back up. She kept moving, with Mrs. Spicklemeyer right in her face until she ran out of floor, her back against the wall.

"Is it really you?" Lucian said, his voice shaking.

Swisbo swayed, and the look on her face was one I'd never seen before. Was it fright?

My dad leapt to his feet and wedged himself between Swisbo and Mrs. Spicklemeyer. I ran to follow him.

"That's enough," he said. "I don't know what's going on here, but you're either mistaken or crazy."

Behind us, I heard someone say, "Get the manager. Now."

"Check this out," a girl's voice said, giggling. "Those two old ladies are going to duke it out."

Even in the midst of all the chaos, I thought, "Boy, Swisbo isn't going to like being called an old lady."

Mrs. Spicklemeyer lunged at my dad, reaching past him to scratch at Swisbo.

"Stop!" I grabbed her arm. She struggled against me, stronger than I'd thought she would be at her age.

But then, the world dropped away.

"Irene?" my mother said. "Lucian?"

CHAPTER EIGHTEEN

Bobbery:
Squabble, commotion, confusion

"You folks are going to have to take this outside or I'm going to call the police." The balding man who had to be the manager gestured toward the door, looking a bit ridiculous in his Western shirt and stiff jeans with his paunch sagging over his out-sized belt buckle. He looked as out of place in the outfit as Abraham Lincoln would look in a onesie. But the two big guys standing behind him looked like the real deal, tough cowboys who could throw a professional wrestler out of a bar if need be.

Ding. I barely heard my phone, riveted on the scene in front of me.

No one moved.

"Lucian?" Swisbo said, her voice shrill. "What are you doing here?"

"We all moved here five years ago. I guess you didn't know, or you wouldn't have dared show your face here." His voice was controlled fury.

"What is going on?" I said.

Lucian turned to look at me and I shrank. The kind face I was used to looked back at me as though I were some hairy creature who had just crawled out of a sewer grate.

"Good question," he said, his voice cold enough to freeze water. "I'd like the answer to that myself."

Ding.

"She knows nothing, Lucian. They know nothing." Swisbo's upper lip beaded with sweat. "Please believe me."

"I don't believe a word that comes out of your mouth." Lucian's jaw tightened.

"Hey," I said, wiggling past Lucian and Mrs. Spicklemeyer to stand with my parents. Swisbo might be many things, but I'd never known her to lie. If anything, she insisted on telling the truth when keeping her mouth shut would be kinder. I didn't know what was going on, but I felt a surge of anger. "Back off."

"Sir? Ma'am? I'm dialing 911 right now." The manager beckoned to the two cowboys, who edged closer, looming over us.

Lucian turned to them and seemed to grow larger. I shuddered. I don't know how I'd ever thought he was grandfatherly. The men took a step back.

The restaurant had grown so quiet that a whisper would have carried across the room. Lucian looked around, seeming to notice for the first time the dozens of eyes glued to the scene.

"I'm coming for you," Lucian hissed at my mother. He took Mrs. Spicklemeyer's arm and pulled. "Let's go," he said to her.

"But..."

"We can't do this here," he said, jerking his head to indicate the crowded restaurant. She nodded, and they walked out of the restaurant into the street.

I looked at my parents. They both looked shell-shocked, which was pretty much the way I felt.

"Mom? Dad?" I said. "What's going on?"

My father snapped out of it first. Ever polite, he said to the manager, "I'm so sorry for the disruption," and he herded my mother and I out into what used to be the lobby of a grand old hotel. He guided us to a green velvet sofa and he and Swisbo sat.

"That was the guy who contacted me about adopting Ariel," my dad said. "Lucian Castlewhite."

My mother didn't say a word.

"Do you know him? What was he talking about? How did you know that lady? Why is she so mad at you? What's going on?" My dad's words ran over each other as he peered into my mother's face.

Ding. I wanted to throw the phone across the room. I reached for it to turn it off, but the messages caught my eye. All of them were from Todd.

"I checked with her parents. Not there." And then:

"Her car is in the parking lot." Followed by:

"Not in study lounge."

Todd was giving me a running commentary of everywhere he had looked. Then,

"Rick says student hit by a car. Calling hospital." My heart skipped a beat.

"Hospital won't give name. Rick said student was female. Going to hospital."

And then, tears sprang to my eyes as I saw the last text.

"It's her."

CHAPTER NINETEEN

QUIETUS:
A FINISHING STROKE; ANYTHING THAT EFFECTUALLY ENDS OR SETTLES

**Sixteen Years Ago: Murder Trial,
Evening before Closing Arguments**

he only light in the paneled office came from a desk lamp which barely made a dent in the gloom. Lucian sat immobile behind his desk, staring out at the starless night and listening to the snow flicking against the window.

"Someone is here to see you," Mrs. Spicklemeyer said from the doorway.

"There's no one I want to see right now," Lucian said, continuing to gaze at the icy landscape.

"I think you'll want to see me," a voice said.

Lucian knew that voice. His head whipped around to the doorway.

"I think I can help your client."

"Achimalech?"

"I need to speak to Lucian privately," Achimalech said to Mrs. Spicklemeyer as he entered the office. She nodded, eyes round, and backed out of the room, closing the door behind her.

"Is it okay if I sit?" Achimalech said, pointing to one of the leather chairs opposite Lucian's desk.

"Be my guest," Lucian said.

Achimalech settled into the chair while Lucian studied him. He'd met Achimalech a few times, but they didn't travel in the same circles. Achimalech was the chief advisor to the leader of the Northern Hemisphere, meaning that he was the second most powerful Descendant in the Northern Hemisphere. He dined on caviar and fine wine with the elite and powerful, while Lucian shared sandwiches with clients accused of reprehensible crimes. Achimalech seemed to always be above the fray, while Lucian toiled smack dab in the middle of the fray. Achimalech didn't come to other people's offices; you went to his office only after an invitation and a thorough security screening.

Lucian couldn't imagine what would bring Achimalech to see him.

"I hear you had a rough day in court today," Achimalech said.

Lucian nodded. He couldn't muster the bravado to deny the crushing blow he and his client had been dealt with the discovery of the light sword.

"I don't know how you come back from that one. I thought your client might have had a chance before, even though slim, but now I don't see any path to a 'not guilty' verdict."

"You've been following the case?" Lucian said.

"Everybody has been following the case." He sighed. "I've known your client for years, and I'm distressed to see him in this predicament."

Lucian snorted. The comment had been so unexpected that he hadn't had time to brace himself to appear stoic.

"I know, I know," Achimalech said, chuckling. "I don't usually extoll the virtues of defense lawyers, but it's guys like you and your client who keep the scales of justice even. I've always thought your client was a good lawyer, fighting the good fight. I don't want to see him taken down by the death of a silly twit who never made a single contribution to our society."

"He didn't kill her," Lucian said.

"Oh, I know, I know," Achimalech said, waving his hand, as though the Defendant's guilt or innocence was of little concern. "But between you and me, I wouldn't blame him for killing her. She was a trouble maker, and I can see how she could drive an old widower crazy enough to do all kinds of things."

Lucian remained silent.

"What do you know of the matters the Defendant was working on in the months before Rachel's death?" Achimalech leaned forward.

This time Lucian had his face under control. He had no idea where Achimalech was going with the question or why he was in Lucian's office, but he had the feeling that he'd just stepped into a poker game with a card shark who had a sixth sense for give-away tells.

"Even if I knew," he said slowly, "I wouldn't be able to tell you. That's covered by attorney-client privilege, not only the privilege I have with my client, but, since we are partners in the same law firm, I'm bound by privilege from revealing any knowledge I obtained about his clients."

Achimalech leaned back, his face smooth, apparently unbothered by Lucian's answer.

"You said 'even if I knew'. Does that mean you don't know?"

Lucian said nothing.

Achimalech cocked his head, scrutinizing Lucian. A beat of silence passed, and Lucian didn't move a muscle, keeping his face neutral.

"It doesn't really matter whether you do or don't know. I believe your client was working on something very important and very confidential. I believe he was acting in what he thought was the best interests of our community. But I believe he was misled."

Lucian's mind raced. What was Achimalech talking about?

"If he agrees to talk to me and tell me everything, I'll make sure he is not convicted."

"You can't promise that. This is a jury trial and – "

"I can make it happen."

"Okay. I'll bite." Lucian's voice held a tinge of sarcasm. "How could you ensure that a jury would find my client not guilty?"

"The 'how' is not important."

"It is to me."

Achimalech straightened, giving Lucian a hard look. Lucian didn't flinch, meeting Achimalech's glare.

"Okay, fine," Achimalech said, leaning back into his chair. "It's simple. The case never gets to the jury."

Lucian raised an eyebrow.

"New evidence could be found. The judge could enter a directed verdict in favor of your client and refuse to let it go to the jury. Or the prosecutor could dismiss the charges."

"What new evidence?"

Achimalech shrugged. "I'm sure we can think of something."

Lucian's face reddened and it was a moment before he spoke.

"I'm not going to be a party to making up evidence."

"Not even to save your client?"

A vein throbbed in Lucian's temple.

"You're never going to win, Lucian, if you don't play by the same rules as the other side."

"What do you mean?"

"Weren't you just arguing today to the Court that it beggared belief that a light sword was miraculously found during trial after your client's home had already been thoroughly searched? What you were really saying, in legal parlance, was that the light sword had been planted. That someone had flaunted the rules to get a conviction, had played God by deciding that your client should be convicted regardless of the trial or the evidence. That someone was determined that the jury find your client guilty regardless of whether he's guilty or not."

Achimalech leaned forward. "It's time to grow up, Lucian. To face reality. This isn't a justice system. It's a pay-to-play, I'll-scratch-your-back-you-scratch-mine, what-outcome-best-serves-our-community system. You can either be a player in it or not. You can spend your life losing 99% of your cases, or you can start to have a fighting chance."

"Get out." Lucian stood.

"Not so fast." Achimalech didn't move. "Aren't you bound to tell your client about my offer?"

"So you use ethical duties when it suits you and discard them when they don't?"

"I'm using your ground rules. If you're going to be the paragon of virtue, then you have to play by those rules. You're required to communicate my offer to your client. He's the one facing a lifetime in prison, not you."

Lucian sat, his mind whirling with thoughts. What was being proposed was unethical and illegal. But who could he report it to? When you rose as high as Achimalech, the only entity you were accountable to was King John IV, the Leader of the Northern Hemisphere, and who knew whether Achimalech was doing this on his own or at King John's behest?

And what would come of reporting it? Achimalech would simply deny that the conversation had ever happened, and Lucian had no illusions as to who would win in that credibility battle.

His brow wrinkled. Did he have an obligation to convey an illegal offer to his client? Lucian wasn't sure, and he had no time to research ethics committee opinions on the matter.

On the other hand, with the discovery of the light sword,

Lucian's suspicion had been confirmed. The trial was rigged. Or, at least, the prosecutor or the investigators or both were willing to plant evidence to guarantee a conviction.

Most of all, Lucian wanted his client to go free. Was it wrong to use illegal means to get an innocent person off when the other side was using illegal methods?

His head throbbed.

"Listen," Achimalech said. "Your only obligation is to convey any offer to your client. It's his call whether to take it or not."

"Actually, that's not true," Lucian said. "If I am part of a conspiracy to do something illegal – which passing on your offer to my client would be – then I'm culpable too. Why don't you just talk to him directly and leave me out of it?"

Achimalech raised an eyebrow. "I assumed you knew. I tried. Lucian refused to put my name on the visitor's list, and when I persuaded the prison bureaucracy to overlook that minor detail and went to see him, the guards had to drag him into the room. He made such a scene that I had to leave. I never got the chance to communicate my offer."

Lucian's mouth fell open. The Defendant had never told him of Achimalech's attempted visit. Lucian had a hard time imagining his client creating such a fuss. On the other hand, he'd never dreamed the Defendant would overturn a table in the middle of a murder trial either.

And why had his client refused to see Achimalech? The Defendant was the type of person who listened to what everyone had to say. The Defendant had met with, and represented, heinous characters. It blew Lucian's mind that the Defendant had refused to meet with Achimalech.

"Why didn't he want to meet with you?"

"Who knows?" Achimalech smoothed his tie. "He's asked for my help in the past on some high profile cases, and I've done what I could. But the past couple of times he asked, I refused to help. Perhaps he still bears a grudge."

Lucian's eyes widened. He couldn't believe the Defendant had had dealings with Achimalech in the past that he had hidden from Lucian. Had they been illegal? Is that why the Defendant had never told him?

He didn't know the answer to those questions, but he needed to find out. He dug in his pocket for an antacid and threw it into his mouth, hoping Achimalech would think it was a mint.

"Okay," he said, feeling like he'd just signed a pact with the devil. "I can't communicate an offer to my client unless I know the details. You're offering him a get out of jail free card in exchange for what? He has had a lot of clients. He was working on dozens of matters at the time Rachel's disappearance derailed his life. Is there a specific one you want to know about, or is it all of them? And what exactly do you want to know about them?"

"He'll know what I want," Achimalech said, standing. "But we don't have much time. I'll make the arrangements right now for you to see your client. You might wait ten minutes before you..." He snapped his fingers. "Oh, that's right. You don't transport." His mouth twitched.

Lucian burned with embarrassment. So everyone knew he couldn't transport.

"I'll have the arrangements made long before you get there in your car, so you better get going."

Lucian stood and pulled his cars keys from his desk drawer.

"I'll be at the jail at 8:30 tomorrow morning to talk to your client," Achimalech said from the doorway.

"But what if he doesn't agree?"

"Oh, he'll agree. He has to know that the light sword was the end of the road for him. He's run his bluff out as far as it will go and now it's time to fold. I'll see you in the morning"

He turned and strolled out.

CHAPTER TWENTY

DISEQUILIBRIUM: A LOSS OR LACK OF STABILITY

"What is it?" Swisbo said. I couldn't believe she'd noticed my distress in the middle of everything else. Or maybe she just wanted the distraction.

"It's Samantha. She's been hit by a car."

"How bad is it?"

"I don't know," I said.

"Well then you better go see her. As quickly as possible," Swisbo said.

"But..." I was torn. Swisbo's face had an ashy tinge. My dad looked distraught. "I don't know if it's serious or not. Maybe she's just there as a precautionary measure."

"No. She's your best friend. You need to go," Swisbo said.

"Which hospital is she in?" my dad said. "We'll take you..."

"There's only one hospital. It's not far." Dad and I rose, but Swisbo put a hand on Dad's arm.

"You take our rental car, Ariel. I need to talk to your dad," she said.

He glanced at her, then did a double take at whatever he saw in her eyes. He sat.

"Call us when you find out what's going on. We'll find our way back to the house. They have Uber here, right?" she said.

I nodded.

"Honey, give her the keys," she told my dad, and he handed them over.

I looked at the keys and then back at my parents. My mother looked hollowed out, like all the energy had been drained from her. My dad sagged back onto the sofa, as though the tensile wire holding him up had snapped. And it probably had. Swisbo is the bedrock our family rests on, and the bedrock had cracked.

"Go," she said, her voice uncharacteristically soft. "We'll be fine. Everything will be fine."

I turned to leave and she grabbed my arm. "Stay around people. Crowds are better. I'll explain later."

My mouth dropped open.

"Now go," she said in a firm voice, freeing my arm and giving me a gentle shove, acting more like the Swisbo I knew.

CHAPTER TWENTY-ONE

Begnornian:
To lament

By the time I got to the parking lot I was gasping for air and it had nothing to do with running. It came from the physical effort of trying to keep panic from bursting through my skin like a tumor, as though the effort of keeping it together was an exercise requiring as much exertion as a half mile sprint.

The earth had shifted under me. Swisbo knew Lucian and Mrs. Spicklemeyer, they obviously hated her, and now might hate me. The guy I'd started to think of as my surrogate grandfather had eyed me as though looking at a tarantula. My bodyguard was MIA and was most likely hobnobbing with her boss, Golgoran, and my best friend had been hit by a car.

Samantha had to be okay. Please let Samantha be okay.

Ten minutes later, I burst into the hospital lobby and the volunteer at the desk directed me to the ICU floor, calling after me,

"Is there someone I can get for you dear? We have a chaplain on staff."

"I'm fine," I said over my shoulder, rushing to the bank of elevators.

I stuffed my breath down in my chest and forced myself to walk normally when I got off on the third floor. I figured they wouldn't want crazy people hovering over patients doing their best to stay alive. I needed to look Buddha-calm, not like a bat-crazy loon.

Two youngish looking men in white coats headed my way, gesticulating widely as they talked.

"Samantha Snelling?" I said, trying to catch their attention.

They didn't even glance my way. "...paged everyone," one of them said to the other. "Surgical teams are on standby. It's a regular organ bonanza."

I hurried on, checking the rooms as I flew by. Most of them seemed empty, and the floor was evening hospital quiet. I rounded the corner and saw a nurse in the hall, entering something on an IPad.

"Do you know what room Samantha Snelling is in?" I said to her.

"And you are?"

I'd watched enough t.v. to know ICU is probably restricted to family only. "Her sister," I said.

"Room 342," she said. "Fifteen minutes only, okay?"

I nodded and turned to find the room. I felt her hand on my arm. "Is there anyone here with you?" I looked up at her. She had kind eyes and a wide body with one of those deep bosoms that made you want to lay your head on her chest. She looked like a comfortable granny from one of the old picture books, the ones they printed before they decided to make all grandmothers skinny so that children wouldn't get the wrong idea and eat too much sugar and fat.

"No," I said.

"Is there someone coming?" she said.

"Yes." I was sure Samantha's parents had to be on their way, and Todd was here somewhere.

"Maybe you should wait – "

"It's okay. I'll be fine. I don't want to waste any time."

She studied my face and then nodded. "I'll take you there," she said and began walking me down the hall toward the room on the end. "I have to warn you, there's been quite a bit of damage."

I nodded, trying to look calm but my stomach rolled. I braced myself as we approached the doorway to room 342 and she gestured for me to go in. I slowly approached the bed, my eyes adjusting to the dim night lighting.

The figure on the bed breathed in and out with the help of a hissing machine mechanically pumping the lungs full of air. A white strip covered her forehead with wires coming out of it, and plastic tubes ran from her arms and snaked out from under the covers. Machines crowded the upper edge of the bed, a mass of green and yellow lights and quiet beeps. The whole thing looked like some kind of modern day Frankenstein scene waiting for the bolt of lightning to bring the patched together creature on the bed to life.

I ripped my eyes from all the flashing lights and forced them to look down at my friend.

I blinked.

"This isn't Samantha," I said. "Are we in the right room?"

The nurse nodded. "Yes, sweetie. I know it's hard to take."

I bent down, examining the patient closely.

Nah. It couldn't be. This lady topped Samantha's weight by at least thirty pounds, and even in the dim light I could see that the face was round, the skin stretched so tight that it looked like it was ready to pop. If I had to guess an age, I'd put her at thirty-two or three, not Samantha's eighteen.

"It's not her," I said, a lilt in my voice.

I know it's shameful, but at that moment, I wanted to high five the nurse, chest bump the doctors in the hall just like Super Bowl football players after the winning touchdown, and go wrap the volunteer at the help desk in the longest hug in history. I didn't care that lying before me was the broken body of someone else's friend, someone else's daughter, someone else's wife or sister or fiancee. It wasn't Samantha, and that's all that mattered.

"I'm sorry honey," the nurse said in a soft voice. "Her body's natural response to the type of injuries she has is to swell, and we've also been pumping her with fluid. I know she doesn't look like herself, but this is your sister."

"Seriously," I said. "This isn't her."

I felt light with relief. Samantha had probably gone over to the bowling alley at the student union. She loved that place. I never could get past the thought of putting on the rented bowling shoes, those fake leather things that nasty feet had sweated in, but that never bothered her. She always snorted, asking me if I was turning into some kind of germ-o-phobe who'd wind up hermetically sealed inside my room Howard Hughes style. I smiled at the memory. When she got back to the dorm, I'd tell her about her near-death experience and we'd laugh ourselves silly.

I turned to face the nurse. "We need to figure out who she is so we can call her real relatives. She shouldn't be alone."

The nurse just looked at me with pitying eyes.

I shook my head impatiently. "I'd know my own fr-sister," I caught myself at the last minute. "She's – "

And then I saw the fingernails. Pink with white peace signs painted on them.

I stared down at the figure and then walked to the foot of the bed and pulled the sheet back from her feet. Blue toenails with white peace signs. My eyes moved back to the face. And as I stared, I finally saw Samantha's features buried under the swelling and the bruises.

I sank into the chair by the bed.

"I'll be back in fifteen minutes," the nurse said, squeezing my shoulder as she left the room.

CHAPTER TWENTY-TWO

STYLITE:
AN EARLY CHRISTIAN ASCETIC WHO LIVED STANDING ON TOP OF A PILLAR

Sixteen Years Ago: Murder Trial, Evening Before Closing Arguments

Lucian rushed through the front door of the jail and approached the front desk, bracing himself for the time-eating rigamarole that the jail personnel delighted in putting him through every time he came. Like making him empty his pockets, go through a full electronic body scan, analyzing the image for long minutes, then insisting on patting him down anyway. On one occasion he'd been forced to strip down to his underwear and wait for thirty minutes in an unheated room while they sifted through his clothes. Defense lawyers weren't beloved by the prison personnel. Anything they could do to dampen Lucian's enthusiasm for visiting his clients, they did.

The officer behind the desk sprang to his feet when he saw Lucian, swiftly removing the toothpick from his mouth and chucking it to the floor.

"Guard," he called. "Open the door for Mr. Castlewhite."

Lucian stared at the officer.

"Guard," the officer yelled again. "Get that door open right now."

The door to where the prisoners were housed flew open.

"Sorry about the delay, sir," the officer said.

Lucian hesitated, waiting for the body scan.

"Go on through. The prisoner is waiting for you."

Lucian turned and walked slowly through the door, wondering if this was a trap and he'd be body slammed to the floor by a 350 pound football lineman turned prison guard.

"Right this way, sir," another officer said, leading Lucian down the hall. Instead of turning left toward the prison cells, he turned right, and escorted Lucian seconds later into a room Lucian had never seen before. Unlike the gray cement floors of the rest of the jailhouse, this room had deep pile carpet. Two leather sofas were arranged opposite each other, flanked by end tables. A decanter filled with amber liquid sat on a walnut table and heavy crystal glasses sparkled next to a gleaming silver bucket filled to the brim with chipped ice, looking so inviting that even a teetotaler would be tempted to have a drink.

The Defendant stood when Lucian entered the room. The officer backed out and closed the door behind him.

"What's going on?" the Defendant said. He gestured at the contents of the room. "How did you arrange this?"

"I didn't," Lucian said. Sweat trickled down the back of Lucian's neck. "Achimalech did."

He'd wrestled with how to put the offer to the Defendant on the drive over, shuffling through dozens of speeches in his mind. He hadn't realized he'd slowed to a crawl until a fed-up driver honked and then flipped him off as he sped by. He'd eased the car over to the side of the road, his hands shaking. Then the realization hit him. He wasn't worried about how to relay the offer. No, he was worried about his client's response. What if the Defendant agreed to reveal confidential information in exchange for his freedom?

Before this night, he'd have bet everything he had that the Defendant would have nothing to do with Achimalech's proposal. But that was before Achimalech had told him that he and the Defendant had had dealings in the past. And, let's face it, the rest of the Defendant's life was on the line. Who knew what one might do to avoid spending the rest of one's life in prison? Lucian would like to believe that the Defendant would be willing to spend the rest of his life in solitary confinement rather than breach his ethics. What if Lucian were wrong? What if the Defendant agreed to the crooked deal?

"Achimalech?" The Defendant's face paled. "What did he say?"

"He said that he could fix the trial in your favor in exchange for you giving him information on a client. He didn't specify which client – he said you'd know what he wanted."

Lucian paused. The Defendant said nothing.

"He also said that you'd worked together in the past." Almost without knowing, Lucian's voice raised at the end in a question. He couldn't bear to know, but he also couldn't bear not to know. If the Defendant had been involved in shady dealings with Achimalech in the past...Lucian swallowed. Was that how the Defendant had bested the prosecutors in the trials he had won? It was rare for a Defendant to win in the Descendants' court system, and the Defendant had won more than his share. Lucian had always thought that the success was due to the Defendant's brilliance as a trial lawyer.

The truth was, the Defendant had always been Lucian's role model. Although the Defendant had tried to talk Lucian out of becoming a defense lawyer, warning him about what a long, lonely road it was to align yourself as the defender of the outcasts, but Lucian couldn't think of anything finer to do. He almost hero-worshiped the Defendant, wanting to be just like him, to fearlessly represent everyone from the innocent to the most heinous criminal. Up until today, Lucian couldn't think of a more ethical person than the Defendant. The word that always came to mind when he thought of the Defendant was "righteous".

But the moment Achimalech had said he'd helped the Defendant in the past, a little bit of Lucian crumbled inside. He couldn't think of any circumstances in which the Defendant would have innocent dealings with someone as high up and as pro-prosecution as Achimalech.

The Defendant sank down heavily on the sofa closest to him.

"Do you know what he wants?" Lucian said. "What client he wants to talk about?"

The Defendant blew out a long sigh. Then he nodded his head.

Seconds ticked by. Still, the Defendant said nothing.

"What do you want me to tell him?"

The Defendant put his head in his hands. After a moment, Lucian heard a murmuring, as though the Defendant was talking to himself. Lucian stepped closer, trying to make out the words.

"...get into this mess...stupid plan...my own fault..."

Finally, the Defendant raised his head. He looked gaunt, and dark circles formed half-moons under his eyes. He rose to his feet.

"Tell him no," he said.

This was what Lucian had wanted to hear - that his hero was still heroic, still one of the good guys, still willing to endure hardship in order to do what was right. But now that he'd heard the answer, the magnitude of the sacrifice almost bent him over with its weight. In that moment, everything changed. He wanted the Defendant to take the deal as much as he'd ever wanted anything in his life.

"Are you sure?" Lucian asked, his voice breaking. "I don't think we have much of a chance of winning after that business with the light sword. You and I both know that it was planted."

The Defendant said nothing, his shoulders slumped.

"Let's think about this." Lucian paced the room. "If they're not playing fairly, why should we? We could - "

"Someone has to hold the line." The Defendant stood, walked over and put his hand on Lucian's shoulder. "If no one does, then we're all lost."

"But do you have to be the one?" Tears shone in Lucian's eyes. "Isn't there someone else?"

The Defendant shook his head. "I've always taught you that the acts of one person can make all the difference in the world – both good and bad."

Lucian's head dropped.

"And Lucian?"

Lucian raised his head.

"I've never had any dealings in the past with Achimalech." He stared straight into Lucian's eyes. After a moment, Lucian nodded.

"Guard," the Defendant called. "I'm ready to go."

Seconds later, the door opened and the Defendant walked out without looking back.

CHAPTER TWENTY-THREE

HOGEN-MOGEN: A PERSON HAVING OR AFFECTING HIGH POWER

"This is your fault you know."

I jumped at the words. I knew that voice. Goosebumps pricked my arms.

Golgoran strolled into Samantha's hospital room, wearing some kind of uniform. I squinted to read the writing stitched over his left breast pocket. The cursive lettering said "Bozeman EMS".

"Yes, I was there," he said. "I helped scrape your friend out of the car and keep her alive while we transported her to the hospital."

I stared at him, dread pressing me down into my chair.

"You seem to be under some impression that you can do what you want without consequences." He gestured toward Samantha's limp form on the body. "You're so, so wrong."

All the slickness that usually oozed from his voice was gone. Golgoran's tone was quiet and dead serious.

Tears filled my eyes.

"You did this?" I could barely get the words out.

He nodded.

"But..." my voice cracked. "She's got nothing to do with this."

He shrugged.

"How can you..." I couldn't finish the sentence. I knew Golgoran and the Enemy were evil. They'd scared me to death over the past few weeks. But I understood why they'd come after me. It made sense because of the crystal I held. I'd felt locked into a battle with them in our own private, nether world that got carried on outside the world of everyone else, like the rest of the population had been marked "safe". The enormity, the lack of care, the pure depravity that the Enemy was capable of hadn't fully registered until this very moment.

I clutched Samantha's hand. I'd put her in this position. My eyes itched from holding back tears.

"I want two things from you," Golgoran said. "And if you agree to those two things, I'll let your friend live."

I stared at him numbly.

"If you refuse, she dies. It's that simple. Do you understand?"

I nodded.

"First, you have to answer this question. How did you escape from your cell? Who helped you?"

"I don't know." My voice quaked.

He shook his head and took a step toward Samantha.

"I mean it," I said, my words tumbling over each other. "Someone just transported me out of there. I never saw him. He was behind me and he was gone before I got a look at him. I didn't recognize the voice. He – or she – used some kind of electronic voice changer. I have no idea who it was. You have to believe me."

Golgoran covered the distance between us in two quick steps and gripped my chin in his hand, forcing me to look straight up into his face.

"You didn't recognize anything? The way he smelled, the way he pronounced words, his choice of words? Think, Ariel." His eyes stared into mine, and I was drawn into them, almost like a victim hypnotized by a swaying cobra.

Seconds passed as I thought back.

"N-nothing was familiar." My words came out slightly muffled since his grip on my chin made speaking difficult.

Golgoran scrutinized me, his hold on my chin tightening until I had to clench my teeth to keep from crying out.

"Okay, I believe you," he said, releasing me. Relief made me lightheaded and I sagged back into the chair.

He walked to the other side of the room and settled against the windowsill.

"Second," he said, "I will save your friend if you come with me and agree to use the Piece of Home exactly as I tell you."

I felt like I'd been punched in the stomach. I'd known in the back of my mind the minute he told me he had two conditions that something like this was coming. Knowing in advance and hearing it out loud were two different things.

"What do you want me to do with it?" My hands twisted in my lap.

"That's above your pay grade. You just have to be compliant. And then when we're done, you can go back to your little life."

I knew exactly what they wanted to do with the Piece of Home. They wanted to use it to gain access to heaven and fight the battle for it all over again.

I looked down at Samantha's swollen face. She was an innocent. She hadn't done anything to deserve to be in this hospital bed.

How bad could it be to go with Golgoran? All kinds of things could happen between now and the time I was required to do something with the Piece of Home. The same guy might rescue me again, or Michael and the Descendants could break me out.

And who says that the Enemy would win the battle if it were

fought again? They lost the first time. I mean, God is in charge of heaven. Surely they couldn't defeat His army. I started to feel a tiny kernel of hope. Maybe I could go with Golgoran, Samantha could live, the Enemy would be defeated and we'd all live happily ever after.

But what if I was wrong? I remembered when I'd first learned about the true power of the Piece of Home from Cyrus and Daniel. They'd been worried, telling me that the Enemy had built up the numbers to win should they ever get the chance to re-enter Heaven.

And the result? Free will – gone. Mankind, if it even continued to exist, being robbed of the ability to make choices, basically being a slave to Satan. What were Daniel's words, "Every shred of goodness or mercy will be immediately stamped out." Did I want to be responsible for that?

But what if I said no and they ultimately got the Piece of Home anyway? Samantha would have died for nothing.

Or, I say yes. Samantha's life is saved. The battle for heaven is lost, and we all become zombies. Including Samantha. Okay, so maybe being a zombie wouldn't be so bad. But would we be zombies? Maybe we'd all be dead? Or maybe we'd be programmed to do evil, repugnant things to each other? I remembered Daniel's words again. "A slow, excruciatingly painful end that will not be complete until well after your lifetime."

My thoughts jumbled together. I now knew what it must feel like if you were trying to defuse a bomb and weren't sure whether to cut the green wire or the red wire.

"Well?" Golgoran said. "What's it to be? I don't have all night."

My head felt like it would split open. I didn't want this responsibility. I hated this responsibility. My breath hitched, and then I was panting, sucking in air as fast as I could, but feeling like nothing was going in. My chest heaved and the room spun. I couldn't catch my breath. Blackness crept in the sides of my vision. "So this is what a horse with blinders on sees," I thought as I swayed in the chair.

"Oh, for Pete's sake," I heard Golgoran's voice say from somewhere far away as he started toward me.

Electric currents seared down the nerves in my arms, running down to my hand like I was being repeatedly hit with a taser. My fingers contracted toward my hands in odd shapes, and I couldn't straighten them out. I stared at my hands in horror. What was happening to me?

Someone moaned from far away. Who was it? Seconds later, I realized it was me, but I couldn't stop. Was I having a stroke? Could a seventeen year old have a heart attack?

Then the pain spread to my lower legs, and I could feel my feet arching and my toes curling up against my boots. I fell out of the chair onto the floor, tears streaming down my face. I'd never felt anything near this level of agony, not even when I'd slammed two of my fingers in a car door.

"What are you doing in here?" a woman's voice from behind me said. "What's the matter with her?"

"I was just walking by and saw that she seemed in distress." I heard Golgoran say.

"Why aren't you helping her?"

"I was just about to," Golgoran said, and I felt him kneel beside me. He bent down until his mouth was even with my ear. He whispered into it, and even in the midst of my misery I shrank from his hot breath on my hair.

"Last chance. Yes or no? Does Samantha live or die?"

"Argh..." I tried again. "Aaargh..." My breath came even faster now, sounding like an old-fashioned locomotive train. I wanted to say yes. I couldn't think about the fate of the world or the millions of faceless people around the world or some celestial battle between good and evil. I knew Samantha. I couldn't let her die. "Aaaaaaargh..."

I couldn't form any words. All that came out of my mouth were garbled moans.

The last thing I saw was Golgoran's awful, empty eyes burning into mine.

And then I blacked out.

CHAPTER TWENTY-FOUR

DESIDERIUM: A FEELING OF LOSS OR GRIEF FOR SOMETHING LOST

I woke feeling blessedly normal. No electric shocks running down my arms, no excruciating muscle cramps, and I seemed to have remembered how to breathe. I held up my hands and blew out a sigh of relief when I saw that they looked normal. I turned my head to find that I was lying on the floor, my head propped up in the nurse's lap.

"Hello," she said. "You're back with us." She smiled down at me.

"What happened?" I said.

And then I remembered Golgoran. "Where'd that man go?" My breath sped up, and just like that my limbs started throbbing again. My fingers began to contort.

"Now you're getting yourself all worked up again. Take it easy. He's gone," she said. "That guy would give anyone the heebie-jeebies.

Now just breathe slowly, honey." She squeezed my hand. "Take a deep breath in and hold it for two counts, then breathe out. On my count, in two three, hold two three, out two three, in two three, hold two three, out two three..."

I followed the metronome of her voice. Almost immediately, the electric shocks subsided. My fingers uncurled.

"That man didn't know a thing about emergency situations." Her voice was sharp. "I'm going to call the EMS and report him. Keep breathing, sweetie. In two three, hold two three, out two three."

"Young man," she said. "Could you get me a wet cloth from the bathroom?"

For the first time I noticed Todd, standing a few feet away. Without a word, he left and seconds later returned with a wet washcloth. The nurse wiped my face with it, and then said, "Are you okay to sit up?"

I nodded. The nurse rose and helped me into the chair. Todd retreated to the doorway and stood, silently watching.

"What happened?" I said.

"It's called hypocalcemia. You were hyperventilating, and when the oxygen level became too low, a calcium transfer happened between your cells which created discomfort in your arms and legs and then caused your fingers and toes to contort. When your breathing still didn't slow down, your body caused you to pass out, which automatically slowed your breathing down and stopped the condition."

I guess discomfort is the medical term for agony.

"Have you had this problem before?"

I shook my head. "I've hyperventilated before, but I've never had – what do you call it - hypocalcemia?"

She nodded.

"It doesn't leave any damage, and is a relatively benign problem," she said.

Easy for her to say.

"I'm guessing that the shock you've had tonight caused the

problem." She laid her hand on my shoulder. "It could happen to anyone. But if it ever happens again, all you have to do is remember to breathe in slowly, hold it a couple of seconds and breathe out. It works almost immediately."

I nodded.

"Okay, dear. You're fine now, but I think you need a break from this room. There's a waiting area at the end of this hall. You can come back in a little while."

"Thank you," I said to the nurse as I stood, the words coming out with far more emotion than I'd expected. What would have happened if she hadn't come in at that moment? Had she bought me more time? I hadn't been able to give Golgoran my answer.

"No problem sweetie," she said. "It happens all the time."

The nurse bustled by me, heading toward another room. I walked to Todd, reaching for him, but he jumped back as though I were radioactive.

"Did you do that to Samantha?" he said, his voice shaking.

"No," I said. Had I? "I mean, I didn't know that..." My voice trailed off.

"I heard that guy. If he can save Samantha...why don't you just do what he wants you to do? What's wrong with you?"

I stood, mute.

Out of the corner of my eye, I saw Samantha's parents rushing down the hall. Todd signaled to them, pointing at the door to Samantha's room.

"Get out." Todd's voice shook. "I don't want you here. Samantha wouldn't want you here if she knew you wouldn't save her."

I couldn't move.

"If she dies, I'm coming after you. Now go," he said, giving me a shove. I stared at him. I don't think I'd ever seen so much hate in someone's eyes.

I slunk down to the waiting room, averting my eyes from Samantha's parents.

Thirty minutes later I heard the code blue. I kept my eyes down, studying the weird bump in the vinyl on the edge of my chair, as though if I didn't look up it wouldn't be real. But I couldn't block out the sound of dozens of feet running down the hall, or the rumble of a hospital bed rolling down the hall, or the buzz of electricity that seemed to ignite the floor.

It didn't take a rocket scientist to figure out what was going on. What had the guy said – an organ bonanza? Harvesting donor organs takes a rapid response time and lots of personnel. The surgical teams were gearing up. Just as I allowed the thought to sink in, I heard Mrs. Snelling's cry. It rang down the hall and stabbed me in the heart.

Apparently Golgoran had taken my non-answer as a "no".

I got up and walked out of the waiting room, down to the lobby, and out into the frigid night. I looked up at the black sky. Even the stars had turned away.

Samantha was gone.

CHAPTER TWENTY-FIVE

GEHENNA:
A PLACE OF EXTREME SUFFERING

Sixteen Years Ago: Murder Trial – Verdict

ucian and the Defendant stood for the jury verdict. They already knew what it would be. Both were lawyers, and both knew what it meant when the jury wouldn't look at you.

"We, the members of this jury," the foreman paused and cleared his throat, "find the Defendant guilty."

A soft cry came from behind the Defendant. Mrs. Spicklemeyer had stood, tears streaming down her face.

The Defendant turned, gazing at her with a look of such love that Lucian had to turn away, feeling that he shouldn't be witnessing something so intimate.

"It will be okay. You will be okay. Lucian will look after you," the Defendant told her.

"Order," the judge said, banging his gavel and glaring at Mrs. Spicklemeyer.

She sat down, covering her eyes.

"The sentence for murder," said the judge in a stern voice, "is either life imprisonment or death. Ordinarily that would be an issue for the jury to decide. However, at the outset of this trial, the prosecutor made it clear that he would not seek the death penalty. Therefore, the Defendant is sentenced to spend the rest of his life in the prison."

Lucian's heart felt as though it had been ripped from his chest. The client put his hand over Lucian's.

"It's okay, son. I'll be fine. Please look after Irene for me," he said, looking back over at Mrs. Spicklemeyer.

Then Lucian watched the man who'd raised him, who'd loved him, and who he loved more than anyone else on earth being hustled out of the courtroom between two armed guards. Lucian's father would spend the rest of his life in the living hell that was the Carcerum Horribilis Penitentiary.

CHAPTER TWENTY-SIX

BUM RAP: A FALSE CHARGE OR FALSE ACCUSATION

I stumbled across the parking lot to my parent's rental car, eyes blurred with tears. Samantha was gone, and it was all my fault. My chest hurt, as though chunks of my heart were breaking off. I had killed my best friend. I'd stolen her parents' only child. Between Mrs. Snelling's Alzheimer's disease and Samantha's death, that had to be more grief than any two human beings could stand.

I wished I'd never come to Bozeman. I wished I'd never met Samantha. I wished I'd never been born.

I opened the car door and sank into the seat. I wiped my face, took a couple of steadying breaths, and fished my phone from my backpack. I shocked myself at the speed dial number my thumb automatically hit. But it was the right number to call. I needed the strongest person I knew right now.

"Please leave a message at the tone." Swisbo's no-nonsense voice echoed in my ear.

My heart sank. I called my dad. Voicemail. I texted both of them. "I'm on my way to the rental house." All I wanted to do was step back into the cocoon of my family, even if they loved my brothers more than me. The quantity of love didn't matter, the fact that they loved me did.

I needed to talk to someone. Michael. It didn't matter that he had bailed on dinner. My snit seemed petty in the context of Samantha's death. I picked up my phone and tried Michael one more time.

"Ariel?"

Thank goodness.

"I've been trying to reach you all day." My voice choked. "You won't believe what –"

"Where are you?"

"I'm at the hospital. Samantha –"

"Don't move. I'm coming to get you." His voice sounded tense.

That was good. I could use a hug. But why did he sound so brusque?

"Is everything – " I started, but then realized that he'd hung up.

What was going on? I called Barnaby. It rang several times and I was about to give up when Barnaby's voice came on the line in a whisper.

"I shouldn't be talking to you."

"What? And why are you whispering?"

"I thought we were friends. How could you not tell me who your mother is?" Even at a whisper, he sounded hurt.

"Huh?"

"Your parents are in custody and your mom is never going to see the light of day. And what about your dad? Was he involved? Why did you really come here? Are you with THEM?" The tone of his voice left no doubt who "them" was – he had to be talking about the Enemy. I'd never heard him sound so serious. He hadn't used a single slang word.

"I don't know what..."

"All I can say is you better tell the truth, because it won't be pretty if you don't. Your mom and dad will eventually talk, and if you don't want to go through what they're going to go through, you need to get out ahead of it."

"Barnaby ..."

"You know, I thought you were my best friend," he said, his voice thick with tears. Then the line went dead.

CHAPTER TWENTY-SEVEN

Filipendulous:
Hanging by a thread

My mind raced, trying to make sense of the last two phone calls. Michael was coming. Barnaby thought I was with the Enemy. My mother was someone - someone bad – that the Descendants knew. My parents were being put through something. A brutal interrogation?

Then my first thought came back. Michael was coming. If Barnaby thought I was with the Enemy, then so did Michael, which explained his terseness on the phone. If Michael came, he'd take me, and I'd probably be in the same position as my parents. A bead of sweat ran down my neck.

I turned off the car. What had my mother said – something about staying around people? Right. I knew enough to know that neither the Enemy nor the Descendants would do anything to me with other people present.

I jumped out of the car, slammed the door and turned to run back into the hospital.

"Hold up." The voice came from behind me.

I whirled. Michael stood three feet away, looking at me like I was a scorpion who'd crawled out from under a rock.

"I..." My throat dried up. I took a step back.

"You're quite an actress. Are you really even adopted? You seem to be a chip off the old block. You fooled me just like your mom fooled everyone. The only thing is, I haven't totally figured out why." His eyes were flinty with dangerous sparks flicking behind them.

"Please believe me Michael. I don't know what you're talking about." My voice came out in a squeak.

"Knock it off." His mouth twisted. "I'm not that stupid."

He took a step toward me and I took another one back.

"Let's go," he said, reaching for me. I sprang away

"Can't we just talk? Tell me what's going on – why you're so angry with me." My voice wobbled.

"I'm not falling for your innocent act anymore. We're going back to the mountain, and you're going to tell me everything you know and everything you've done."

After what Barnaby had said about what my parents would 'go through', I didn't want to go back to the mountain. I was afraid I'd never come out.

I glanced around. No vehicles drove through the parking lot, no family headed toward their cars after visiting loved ones. It was just me and Michael. I peered at the glass doors of the hospital entrance. I didn't see anyone but there had to be someone just inside those doors.

I looked back at Michael.

"Let's go," he said, stepping toward me.

I whirled and ran toward the hospital entrance, my backpack bouncing with each step.

I'd only gone a few yards when hands grabbed me from behind, lifting me off the ground. My arms flailed, trying to connect with Michael, but hitting someone from that position is almost impossible.

I started to feel the familiar electric buzz that comes right before the loosening of cells, and knew I was seconds from being transported. Out of the corner of my eye I saw a large round circle jutting out from a light post. I wrenched my body, bucking toward the right, slapping at the air, trying to hit the red circle. I was still too far away.

I kicked backwards, using the heels of my cowboy boots to aim at Michael's shins, pounding as hard as I could. His grip loosened and I kicked harder, pummeling him. Michael dropped me and my feet hit the ground.

I leapt toward the light pole and the precious red button but Michael grabbed my arm, jerking me back. I stomped on his foot, just like in the self-defense class Swisbo had signed me up for and Michael's hand loosened. I pulled away from him, reaching for the red button. The tips of my fingers grazed its edge and I pushed.

Nothing.

I stretched as far as I could, straining for the button. This time, I managed to hit it with my palm.

Still nothing.

Just as Michael's grip tightened, I stretched again, feeling something pull in my side. I bit off a groan and smacked the button as hard as I could. A red light swirled on the side of the light pole and a loud, obnoxious beeping tore at my eardrums sounding like a car alarm, only magnified times three. After the fourth beep a mechanized voice said, "Stop. You are under surveillance. Security guards are coming. Your actions are being recorded."

Michael let me go and stepped back.

"Beep. Beep. Beep. Beep. Stop. You are under surveillance. Security guards are coming. Your actions are being recorded. Beep. Beep. Beep. Beep."

Michael's fists clenched and he stared at me, his eyes so cold that they froze me in place.

"Beep. Beep. Beep. Beep. You..."

He shook his head and then backed away until he was outside the pool of light, and disappeared.

CHAPTER TWENTY-EIGHT

EUREKA: I HAVE FOUND IT

The police station was a disappointment. I'd been picturing gritty floors and beat up desks, harassed detectives in suits that looked like they'd been slept in, buzzing on caffeine and adrenaline, and maybe a perp or two being hustled in by beefy patrolmen. Instead, it looked more like a real estate office.

A lanky patrolman sat on the edge of a desk, debating the odds of the Grizzlies beating the Bearcats with a man dressed in a white shirt, tie and slacks sitting behind a scrupulously clean desk. Sure, the tie was loosened, but the shirt was crisp and the tie looked brand new. As I walked by the pair, a faint aroma of after shave wafted in my direction.

A security guard had arrived within seconds of Michael's departure, and he'd called the police. Within minutes, two patrol cars had arrived and had searched the area for what they all assumed was a kidnapper/rapist. They'd studied the security video and had seen Michael grabbing me and my attempts to get away. I'd agreed (actually, I'd begged) to be taken to the police station to file a report and had been turned over to Detective Davis, a slow-talking, methodical man who shared my love of dogs but took fishing way too seriously.

I'd been basically truthful, other than the fact that I'd told him I'd never seen the man who grabbed me before and that I had no idea why he'd come after me. Oh, and that the brief conversation we'd had was him asking me for money and me telling him I didn't have any. And that my parents were on a trip to Argentina and I couldn't reach them. And that the reason I had no one to stay with me was that my roommate had gone home to see her parents in Idaho.

Okay, basically truthful might be an overstatement.

I hadn't cried until Detective Davis had pressed me for the name of a friend who I could go and stay with for the night. I'd barely said the name "Samantha" before I cracked, and Detective Davis had patiently waited while I sobbed my way through the story of the car accident, handing me tissues.

I'd sounded pathetic enough that he'd told me I could hang out at the station for the rest of the night until I could reach my parents or my roommate. I figured neither the Enemy nor the Descendants would try anything at a police station, and at the very least, I would have people around me all night long. He'd shown me into a room with a couch and a Keurig coffeemaker, and told me to make myself at home.

"Would you like me to close the blinds?" he asked, pointing to the glass wall looking out into the desk area. A patrol officer had joined the Cats/Grizzlies discussion.

"No." My voice came out somewhere between a shriek and a scream. If I couldn't see out, no one could see in, which meant Michael or Golgoran or who knows who could transport in at will and take me.

"How about if I leave the door open too. Is that okay?" Detective Davis said. I could tell he was trying to keep his voice as calm and soothing as possible, probably afraid I'd go into full girl hysterics at any moment.

I nodded.

"I'll be right out here if you need anything."

"Thank you." Detective Davis was quickly turning into my hero.

I drew my knees up and hugged them to me. Now what? If it were possible to take a picture of the thoughts in my brain, it would have looked like an exploding bomb, bits and pieces flying everywhere. I had no plan, and I needed a plan.

Samantha. Tears welled in my eyes again. I brushed at them roughly. I didn't have time to mourn Samantha right now. My family might be joining her if I couldn't figure a way out of this situation.

My mind raced. I had to get my parents out of the mountain. I had to stay out of the clutches of the Enemy and the Descendants. I had to keep the Piece of Home from falling into the wrong hands. I had to...

The faintest thread of an idea broke through the chaos in my head. The Piece of Home. It was the key to everything. I was only in this mess because of the Piece of Home. What are the odds that the Descendants are interested in me because of the Piece of Home and are interested in my parents for a totally different reason? It had to be tiny, like one in a billion.

I unfolded from my fetal crouch and sat forward on the edge of the sofa. I even knew the formula to calculate those odds, courtesy of Intro to Statistics, the second most boring class after Intro to Logic. To find the probability of two independent events occurring at the same time, you multiply the probability of one by the probability of the other:

$$P(A) \cdot P(B) = P(A \text{ and } B)$$

Slight problem. I have no way to know what the probability of either A or B are in this scenario. And when I'm figuring it out, do

I include the fact that I have the Piece of Home? I mean that would change the value of A significantly, as in there is 100% probability that the Descendants would be interested in me if you factor in that I have the Piece of Home. Likewise, the parents of the person holding the Piece of Home; i.e. B, would be of interest, although not as much as A, but if you took out the Piece of Home factor then the odds would be a billion to one, which if multiplied by...

My head ached. I gave myself a mental scolding. I didn't need a math formula. The two had to be related.

I sat up, an idea edging through the confusion in my brain. There was a way to get me and my family out of this situation and ensure that there'd be no reason for the Enemy or the Descendants to bother us again. Up until now, I'd been relying on others to guarantee our safety. I sighed. That ship had definitely sailed. But I could guarantee my family's safety by doing one thing myself.

I had to destroy the Piece of Home.

"I thought..."

I shrieked.

"I didn't mean to startle you." Detective Davis hovered in the doorway.

"Sorry, I'm just a little freaked." My face burned.

"I understand. I just thought you might want something to take your mind off of things." He walked over to me as though approaching a skittish pony and handed me a book with a blue cover. I turned it over. The title read, *We Don't Make This Stuff Up – The Very Best of the Bozeman Chronicle Police Report.*

I looked up at him.

"Seriously, you should read it. When people have been through a shock like you have, sometimes it helps just to think about something else for a while." The corners of his eyes crinkled in a half smile.

"Thank you," I said, smiling back. "I'll try it."

"I'll check on you later," he said, and left the room.

I cracked open the book, and began leafing through it, my mind still focused on my problem. Yes, the idea would work but I had one tiny problem.

If the Descendants and their team of super nerds couldn't figure out how to destroy the Piece of Home, how was I supposed to?

A man in the 700 block of Mountain View Drive complained because his girlfriend's husband kept stopping by. September 8, 1997

On the other hand, had they really been trying to figure out how to destroy it? It seemed like most of their efforts had been geared toward trying to get the Piece of Home away from me.

A patrol car collided with an animal on Amsterdam Road. The suspect was identified as "Doe. A deer. A female deer." November 18, 1994

I didn't need a probability formula to figure out the odds that I could crack the secret of destroying the Piece of Home. I'd put it at somewhere less than .0000001%. A sickening realization hit me. Since it was actually a piece of heaven, it might be impossible to destroy at all.

A husband and wife had an argument. The wife later took some cash from the house. The husband said he was planning to use the cash to pay bills; the wife said she was planning to use it to hire a divorce lawyer. April 6, 2008

A man was stopped on suspicion of drinking while driving. He denied having any alcohol, but was unable to provide an explanation for the six-pack of

beer with three empty cans frozen to the top of this car. January 8, 2014

Despite myself, the corners of my mouth turned up. I flipped back to the front of the book and read the foreword. Yes, these were actual reports called into the Bozeman Police Department by Bozeman residents. I went back to my place in the book.

A man reported he thought a bobcat was under his porch. Also, his cat was missing, which he thought could be related. October 12, 2013

A man called asking if he could file assault charges against his ex-fiancee who had given him a black eye when she tried to scratch a mirror with her engagement ring and found out it wasn't a real diamond. He was advised that he could either file charges or spring for a real diamond. September 8, 2012

I wondered what kind of stone had been in the woman's ring. During my brief love affair with rocks, I'd charted the properties of different stones and had carried around a Mohs testing kit my dad had bought for me which enabled me to determine the hardness of different rocks as part of the identification process.

I knew that diamonds were on the top end of the hardness scale with a Mohs value of 10, and I'd learned that cubic zirconia was almost as hard, making a scratch test unreliable for telling a real diamond from a cubic zirconia. Had the guy gotten her a polished quartz?

My hand fingered the Piece of Home hanging around my neck. I wondered what its Mohs scale hardness was.

I sat upright. If I knew what the Piece of Home was made of, then maybe I could figure out how to destroy it. And if I destroyed it, none of these un-angelic creatures would have any interest in me or my family anymore.

I pulled my mom's logbook out of my backpack. She was the one who'd found the Piece of Home after all. It seemed like every time she saw a formation she took a sample of it, analyzed it, and wrote down its formula. Maybe in all those dry pages she'd figured out the chemical makeup of the Piece of Home. Now that I knew what to look for, maybe I could get through the dense writing. I flipped, running my fingers down each page.

Crap. There were a lot of formulas.

Flip and google. For the next hour, that's all I did. I'd see a formula, google it and move on. Turns out my bio mom liked to use the chemical formulas instead of the names.

Who does that?

Like she'd say "Unexpected deposit of SiO2 at upper elevations," which turned out to be rose quartz. I wondered if I could get extra credit in chemistry for my burgeoning knowledge of the chemical composition of rocks and minerals.

Then I saw some figures that looked familiar:

X = MOHS > 10

C(s): 1274 - -1544F→C(g)

C(s): 10 GPa + 8540.33→C(l)

EC = 12992-1598

GPa @ OC > 130

My skin tingled. The 7 had a dash through the middle, just like the figure in my jail cell at the Enemy's headquarters. I was sure that these were some of the same numbers I'd seen in the cell.

A nasty thought crept into my brain. Goosebumps bristled on my arms. Was it possible that my mother had been a prisoner in the same cell where I had been? Had she been the one who'd written those formulas on the cell wall?

I swallowed. It almost had to have been her.

It looked like my bio-mom was trying to figure out "X", and whatever "X" was had a hardness on the Mohs' scale of greater than 10. I didn't know what the heck the other numbers and symbols meant, but I had a cold certainty of one thing: she'd been trying to determine what the Piece of Home was made of. My eyes pricked with tears. We were thinking alike!

Then another thought pushed its way into my head and my stomach lurched. Was the faint odor of death lingering in the cell from her? I swallowed hard, trying not to gag. I didn't have time to think about that right now.

I sucked in a deep breath. It didn't help. I clapped a hand over my mouth, trying not to throw up. Images of a dark-haired, petite woman who looked like me frantically scratching away at the cell walls, knowing death was coming, jumbled through my mind. Had she been afraid?

Of course she had. She'd probably been terrified.

I shook myself. This wasn't helping. Something from my high school psych class tickled at the back of my mind. Oh yes, that was it. Compartmentalization: a subconscious psychological defense mechanism used to avoid the mental discomfort and anxiety caused by a person's having conflicting emotions within themselves. I needed some good old compartmentalization right about now.

I shoved the image of my mother deep into the back of my mind. My psych professor had been big on visualization, so I actually pictured me escorting her to the back of my brain and leaving her there.

I bent over the figures in the logbook, trying to concentrate. For an instant I had a vision of all the things I'd shoved to the back of my mind in the last few hours – Samantha's death, Todd's anger, Michael's coldness, Lucian turning against me, the mystery of Swisbo knowing Lucian and Mrs. Spicklemeyer, Rosamund's betrayal. The back of my mind might as well have a neon 'No Vacancy' sign blinking at its entrance. I didn't know how much more I could stuff back there without the whole thing exploding.

I was sure the formulas had to be related to the Piece of Home. I was also sure that my bio-mom had been killed by the Enemy because of the Piece of Home. If I didn't want to join her, I had to figure out how to destroy it, once and for all.

I could only take so much reality at one sitting. I shoved the logbook into my backpack and got up to see if the Keurig machine had any hot chocolate pods.

That's when it happened. Lights blinked outside in the parking lot, and I watched as the lights on the tall poles illuminating the lot winked out one by one.

Then every light in the police station went out.

CHAPTER TWENTY-NINE

Besiege:
Surround (a place) with armed forces in order to capture it or force its surrender

"What the heck?" Voices rumbled outside the door. "Someone go check the circuit breakers."

I jumped to my feet, the skin prickling on the back of my neck. I found the flashlight app on my phone, put the logbook in my backpack and shrugged it on.

"Ariel?" Detective Davis stood in the doorway. "Everything is okay. It's probably just a tripped circuit."

I guess it's possible to trip every circuit in the place at the same time. Or maybe the main circuit breaker had blown. But the way my day was going, I didn't think so.

"We should have the lights back on any second." He turned to leave.

"Could you stay with me?" My voice quivered.

"Uh, sure," he said. "No problem."

He walked over and sat down in a chair, and I perched on the arm of the couch, too uneasy to settle into a full sitting position. As long as he stayed with me, I was pretty sure that no one would try to snatch me.

"Has this happened before?"

Detective Davis stared at me blankly.

"You know," I swiveled my head around the dark station, "the power going off?"

"Yeah, the power goes off a lot around here and it's worse in the winter. They'll have it back on in no time."

My stomach fluttered. No matter what Detective Davis said, I couldn't shake the feeling that someone or something was hovering just out of sight, waiting to catch me alone.

I saw a flashlight bobbing down the hall towards our room, met by another flashlight coming from across the hall.

"Find anything?" I heard one of them ask.

"Nope," the other one said. "None of the circuits are tripped. I called Northwestern Energy and they're not showing a power outage around here."

My heart began beating in triple time. I stood.

"It's okay, Ariel," Detective Davis said. "They always say they don't show a power outage."

"Hey Nathan," he called to one of the figures behind the flashlights. "Is Northwestern going to send someone?"

"They said they would, but you know them – they're never in a hurry."

My head swiveled to look out the window. It had been clear when I'd walked into the police station. As if on cue, the windows rattled as wind gusted against the panes. Even in the dark, I could see that what had been a tranquil night had turned into a wall of snow, not the fluffy kind depicted on postcards, but whip-sharp needles of icy pellets blasting through the air as though catapulted from a turbo-charged leaf blower.

The wind picked up, making an eerie whistling sound. The windows shook, pummeled by snow, rocks, debris, anything the wind could scoop up from the parking lot and surrounding trees.

"Boy, this is a doozey," Detective Davis said, looking unconcerned. "I'm glad we're in here and not out there." He tapped a button on his phone, and cupping his hand over the bottom of it said, "The wife's a little spooky. I'm just going to check on her."

I nodded.

"Hon," he said a second later, and then after a pause, "No, I'm not coming home yet. I have a little work to finish but I thought I'd check on you. Are you weathering the storm?"

I heard sounds from the phone but couldn't make them out. Detective Davis shook his head.

"No, I mean the wild snow storm outside." The phone light glowed against his face, and his brow furrowed. "Really? We've got a whopper going on here." More sounds came from the phone, and then he said, "Well, don't go anywhere. It's a bad storm and it could be heading your way. All right. I'll be home as soon as I can."

"That's weird," he said, turning to me. "I guess we're just in the wrong place. My wife says it's clear and calm at the house."

"How far away do you live?" I said.

"Just over in Valley West, about two miles from here."

The flutters in my stomach melded into a hard knot.

A terrific crash sounded over my head. I jumped, stifling a shriek.

"I think that was a tree limb." Detective Davis had gotten to his feet too. "Must have come off in the wind. Everything is all right." But he remained standing, peering out into the swirling storm beyond the window. I followed his eyes, just as a limb shattered the window like a javelin, missing my head by inches.

I sprang back and fell to the floor. Glass flew through the air, propelled by the vicious wind. I covered my face and curled into a fetal position, trying to protect myself from the shards. The temperature dropped from toasty to icy as the wind invaded the room. I shivered, not so much from the cold, but from a growing certainty that the storm had nothing to do with Mother Nature.

"Ariel?" It was Detective Davis' voice, yelling over the roar of the wind. "Crawl to the door. We've got to get out of the room."

I couldn't move. The Enemy was out there. Or was it The Descendants? It could be either one. And they had caused this storm for one reason – to get me.

I suddenly understood the whole deer in the headlights analogy, where the deer sees the car coming and stops in the middle of the road, its muscles frozen in fear, unable to move even though death is speeding towards it behind the headlights of a four-wheeled metal bullet.

"Ariel. You have to move. The wind keeps picking up the glass. You're going to get hurt." His arm tugged at my sleeve.

"I'm c-coming," I said, hoping it was true. I wanted to, but my muscles seemed to have stopped working, like a frozen computer that needs to be rebooted. My brain said, "go, go, go!" but my body refused to move.

For some bizarre reason, my mind flipped back to my Liebniz's theory in my Logic class. Had it only been that morning? Something about God being all powerful, blah, blah, blah – and this part I remembered with vivid clarity – 'ergo, this is the best of all possible worlds.'"

Liebniz was a total idiot.

CHAPTER THIRTY

COMMINATORY: THREATENING, VENGEFUL, PUNITIVE

At the Descendants' Headquarters in the Mountain

he room could have been a cozy den in any one of her neighbors' homes, with recessed lighting, deep couches, and a fire crackling in the fireplace. But Swisbo knew better. The walls looked normal, but upon close inspection were made of a material that looked as soft as a marshmallow. She wasn't going anywhere, like a firefly trapped in a mason jar.

The door opened and Lucian entered with two men.

"Where is my husband?" Swisbo said.

No one answered as the three advanced upon her.

"What have you done to him?"

Still no answer.

"I'm not telling you anything until I know he is okay." Her voice was loud.

"I don't need you to tell me anything," Lucian said, his voice tight.

The two men grabbed Swisbo and before she could react, Lucian yanked a tuft of hair from her head. They released her just as quickly.

"This is all I need," he said, pulling a plastic zip lock bag from his pocket and placing the hair inside. "And once the lab tells me what I already know—"

"I want to hire you as my lawyer," she said, reaching to put a hand on his arm.

He jerked away as though he'd been bitten by a rabid dog.

"Please, Lucian. Please help me." Tears flooded her eyes.

"You are finally going to pay for the lives you have ruined. I would not help you if my life depended on it. In fact, I'm going to do everything in my power to help the prosecutor make it so that you never see the light of day again." He glared at her.

"But you don't understand. Ariel –"

He waved his arm, cutting her off.

"Ariel will be found and we will get to the bottom of all of this. Even though she's adopted, it looks like you have trained her well. She had me totally fooled, just like you fooled everyone. But right now, all I care about is getting to the court with this proof." He held up the zip lock bag.

"I would never have let her come here if I'd known –"

Lucian spun on his heel and the door slammed behind he and the two men as they left.

Swisbo sank down onto the sofa, burying her head in her hands. She'd been so careful, so vigilant. She'd remade herself into some-one unrecognizable from the girl she'd been. She'd done every-thing she was supposed to do.

How had it gone so wrong?

CHAPTER THIRTY-ONE

Cacophony: A harsh discordance of sound

Hands tugged at my arms, and I felt myself being pulled through the scrum of wind, glass, snow and ice. Seconds later I was sitting on the floor behind the cover of one of the desks in the center of the police station. Detective Davis sat beside me, tiny rivulets of blood running down his face.

One of the flashlights ran up, panting, and said, "I got the door closed, so the glass is contained. Are you okay, Davis?"

"I'm fine Nathan – just little nicks. Check on her, would you?"

Nathan bent down and his flashlight momentarily blinded me. I covered my eyes.

"Sorry," he said.

"I'm fine," I said. That was a canard, but physically I was fine. Mentally...let's just say I could see a padded room in my future if I didn't pull it together.

"Are you sure?" he said.

I nodded.

His knee joint cracked as he straightened up. He rubbed it absently and then his hand stopped. All three of us stared at each other, all hearing the same thing.

Nothing. No wind, no rain, just an unnatural, dead silence.

The arms bristled with goosebumps and the ends of my hair starting floating free as though struck by static electricity. Then the silence was broken.

One bass drum beat a slow dirge, joined by another, and then another, the sound surrounding us, seeming to come from everywhere. Seconds later, an urgent staccato rhythm layered on top of the bass drum. The air throbbed with the drums' almost military beat, growing so loud that I felt it inside my chest, as though the cadence had insinuated itself into my own heartbeat.

Then the sound got worse. Trumpets wailed over the drumbeats in a totally different rhythm. I'd never heard a call to battle but this had to be one. The drums beat harder, as though fighting the trumpets, who, in return blared even louder. My hands flew to my ears, covering them from the awful din.

If terror had a sound, it would sound like this.

Nathan nudged Detective Davis and pointed to the windows. I followed their gaze.

Two moving rings swirled around the outside of the windows, apparently circling the building - one moving clockwise, and the other counter-clockwise. One was made up of drums, the other of trumpets. No forms could be seen, just the musical instruments circling in a slow, ominous spiral.

The words to a Bible song I'd learned as a kid came to mind. "Joshua fought the battle of Jericho and the walls came tumbling down." It had stuck with me because as detailed in the Old Testament, the Israelites had marched around the supposedly impregnable walls of their enemy Jericho for six days, blowing their trumpets, the first recorded instance of psychological warfare.

On the seventh day, the Israelites marched around the walls seven times, and then the stone walls had collapsed. I'd had a Sunday School teacher who'd taken a little too much pleasure in describing the growing terror the people inside the walls must have felt minute after minute, hour after hour, day after day, bombarded by the sounds of marching and trumpets, knowing an attack was coming but not knowing when.

"Call all units back to the station," Detective Davis said, yelling above the noise. "Apprise them of the situation and tell them to approach with caution."

"They're never going to believe me," Nathan said, his face pale above the flashlight's beam.

I hated to tell them, but the entire Marine Corps wasn't going to make a difference. I knew what this was about. My guess was that the Descendants and the Exiles were amassed outside, both trying to get to me first.

I felt something land on my forehead. I looked up and another tiny object hit my face. I grabbed Detective Davis' flashlight and pointed it upward.

A tiny crack grew in the ceiling above us. As we watched, it lengthened, stretching towards the ends of the building. Pieces of debris flaked off, falling onto the floor, and the crack started widening.

My ears popped as the pressure changed in the building. The building shrieked as the crack grew from inches to three feet.

"We've got to get out of here," Nathan said. "It's coming apart and we're going to get buried in it when it falls."

"You're right. Back door?" Detective Davis said, grabbing my arm.

Nathan nodded. We ran, with Nathan leading the way. My brain scrambled for a plan as we hustled through the main bullpen to a corridor. Outside wasn't going to be any better for me than inside. I was doomed either way. On the plus side, I guess if we went outside at least the building might be saved. If I was no longer in it, there'd be no reason to rip it apart.

We came to the end of the hall and pushed open the door. It was rigged with a fire alarm, but the noise outside drowned it out. The booming drums and blaring trumpets almost burst my eardrums.

Within seconds after we stepped outside, the circles stopped swirling and the din stopped. I stared at the suspended instruments, waiting for whatever was to come next.

Seconds passed. Nothing happened. Both Detective Davis and Nathan stood frozen. I could almost see the wheels churning inside their heads, trying to make sense of the spectacle in front of them.

Two figures appeared just inside the circle, walking together. One was dressed in red armor; the other in black. It was modern, tactical armor, not the kind you see in old fairy tales, but it had a slight sheen to it, as though it was glowing from within. Full face helmets hid their features. They stalked toward us, and I involuntarily backed up. Arms reached out – one figure grabbed Detective Davis, the other took Nathan.

"No..." Detective Davis yelled, and then both were lifted up and disappeared along with the figures holding them.

I was left alone in the middle of the circle.

I saw movement and then blurred objects behind the circle of instruments. I rubbed my eyes, and then turned, letting my eyes take in what was happening in front, behind and to the side of me. Figures appeared – row after row, neatly divided down the middle of the circle between red and black, each soldier illuminated by the faint glow of their armor.

Then the holders of the instruments materialized. The drummers wore white vests and pants trimmed in gold, with red flowing capes held by gold epaulets from their shoulders. Their arms were corded with muscle. The trumpeters wore black from head to toe, with gleaming ebony boots riding up to their kneecaps. The sole dash of color came from silver buttons on their shirts, matching the silver instruments in their hands.

Seconds passed in utter silence, but the silence pulsated with tension. Something bad was going to happen. I looked around for a way out but all I could see was the black asphalt of the parking lot under my feet, with all possible escape routes cut off by the circle of musicians and soldiers.

Out of the corner of my eye I caught a flash of light. Then a trumpet blew and chaos broke out. The battle – for that's what it had to be – had begun.

I shrank to the ground, covering my head. The screaming coming from all sides finally forced my eyes open. I couldn't stand not knowing what was happening. My eyes widened.

No drone strikes or sniper shots from hidden towers struck, and no missiles fired from distant tanks. This was hand to hand combat with shrieks and howls and cursing and crying. As I watched, a black clad soldier bulldozed a red armored soldier, knocking him to the ground. He then stood on top of him and used his light sword to work on the neck of the full-face helmet where it connected to the body armor, like some kind of a metal cutter. The soldier on the ground kicked and rolled, managing to topple his attacker off of him. They grappled on the ground, and then I lost sight of them in the cauldron of light swords, moving arms, legs and bodies.

The drums boomed and the trumpets wailed. I covered my ears, trying to block out the awful noise, but it was too loud. I caught a glimpse of a body with no head, and then another, and another. The sights and sounds caved in on me, and I couldn't move, as though I'd been shocked to my spot.

A sea of black appeared behind the chaos, surrounding the fighters as far as my eye could see. Before then, the numbers of the two sides had seemed almost equal, but that had been a momentary illusion. The soldiers in black outnumbered the red clad soldiers by at least ten to one.

I didn't know which side was which. Were the black clad soldiers the Enemy? Or was that the red armored soldiers?

The drummers and trumpeters disappeared as the circle around me shrank. Their atonal music – if you could call it that – continued, but they'd given way to the soldiers, all seeming to have one purpose – to get to me.

I had no where to go. The soldiers were now so close that I could feel the heat from the light swords. I saw fewer and fewer red soldiers, the black clad soldiers enveloping them like a remorseless sea, destroying everything in its wake. A red clad arm burst through the black tide and grabbed me.

"Ariel," said a familiar voice, panting.

I peered through the eye slits.

"Cyrus?"

"We've got to go," he said.

I hesitated. I knew the Enemy were the bad guys and I didn't want to go with them. But were the Descendants the good guys? After all, they were holding my parents prisoner and didn't seem interested in destroying the Piece of Home.

"Come on Ariel." Cyrus pulled on my arm. "Quickly, before it's too late."

Still, I hesitated. Sounds of battle roared around me, cries of effort, screams of pain, the drums beating louder and louder. I couldn't think. But what choice did I really have?

I reached out with my other arm and grabbed Cyrus. I felt the buzz of electricity, the loosening of cells, the blurring of my vision that told me we were about to transport.

Cyrus' grip loosened.

My vision cleared. Three black clad warriors pulled on Cyrus, wresting him away from me. My hands slipped from his arms.

The warriors threw him to the ground. One of them bent and twisted Cyrus' helmet off.

Cyrus' eyes met mine. He looked strangely calm.

"Don't ever give it to them, Ariel," he said. "No matter what."

A light sword raised in the air and arced down towards Cyrus' neck.

"No!" I cried.

And then a black gloved hand yanked me away, pushing me into the arms of two hulking figure, their faces anonymous behind their black helmets.

"Take her to the Control Center," a harsh voice said. "I'll clean up here."

Then everything went black.

CHAPTER THIRTY-TWO

DISENTHRAL:
TO SET SOMEONE FREE

In the Carcerum Horribilis Penitentiary

ucian had no idea what to expect. He hadn't seen his father in seventeen years since the terms of his sentence didn't allow any visitors, even relatives. Lucian braced himself to see a broken man.

Lucian walked down the gray corridors with Judd Preston, aka "No Body No Problem", the prosecutor who had put his father, Zachariah Castlewhite, in this place. Judd kept patting Lucian's arm, ordering guards to move "like your pants are on fire or you'll be looking for a new job", and generally acting like Lucian's new best friend.

Lucian wasn't fooled. His dad's case had made Judd's career - getting a murder conviction of a respected lawyer despite the fact that no body had ever been found. It was the stuff of legends. Lucian guessed that Judd could now see his career nosediving as swiftly as it had skyrocketed.

Lucian had taken the hair he'd yanked from Swisbo's head straight to the crime lab to have the DNA matched to evidence he'd kept from the trial, not because he had any doubt, but because he knew the court would require it. He'd told Judd the news, who had joined with him in assembling an emergency hearing within the hour where both he and Judd had asked the court to release Lucian's father immediately.

Lucian shook off Judd's arm. Ever since his father's trial, Judd had looked at Lucian as one might look at a scroungy dog who'd been hit by a car and left whining by the side of the road, with a mixture of pity and disgust. Judd's new-found fawning attention irritated Lucian to the core.

After his father had been sent to prison, Lucian had quit associating with any of the Descendants except for work. When the Descendants decided to move from Denver to make Bozeman, Montana their new headquarters five years ago, he'd come with them, but hadn't moved into the mountain. He was popular with criminal defendants because, unlike all the other defense attorneys, he could be persuaded to believe a good conspiracy theory. Planted evidence, lying prosecutors, crooked judges – Lucian was likely as not to believe it, and his sheer belief made him a formidable opponent. There's nothing more convincing than a true believer, and Lucian's honesty and passion, especially emanating from such a seemingly mild-mannered man, made him a persuasive advocate.

But the toll had been heavy. He'd never married, had no social life or friends other than Mrs. Spicklemeyer and grateful clients, and dedicated his life fully to his work, as though wearing the hair shirt of his father's conviction required him to eschew any semblance of a normal life.

It wasn't the future he'd envisioned for himself.

That woman had not only ruined his father's life, she had reduced his to a shell of what it might have been.

They rounded the last corner and the hall dead-ended into a dingy wall embedded with a door, remarkable only in the fact that both the door and the wall looked a bit like a stuffed mattress. Lucian knew that they were made of a material that prohibited the occupant from transporting anywhere. The person behind those walls was grounded.

The guard pulled out a ring of keys, fumbling through them.

"Hurry up you idiot," Judd said.

The ring slipped through the guard's fingers and clanked to the floor.

"Do I have to do this myself?" Judd said, glaring at the guard.

"No, sir. I've got it." The guard grabbed the ring from the floor, flipped through several, and then selected a gold key and put it in the lock. The door swung open.

Lucian stepped inside, taking in the windowless room. A cot took up one whole side of the small room, and a small sink and toilet monopolized the other side of the room. Squeezed in between them, sitting on the floor cross-legged in a classic lotus yoga pose was a white-haired man. He sprang to his feet, moving with an agile grace.

Lucian's mouth dropped open. Was this his father? The man seemed to have his father's face, but looked twenty years younger than the last time Lucian had seen him.

"Lucian?" his dad said. "Is that you?"

"Dad?" Lucian reached for him and the two men met, hugging hard. Tears rolled down Lucian's face. He'd dreamed of this moment for years, but hadn't believed it would ever happen. He held on tight, never wanting to let go.

His dad was the first to loosen his grasp. "Are you all right? What's going on? Why are you here?"

"We've found Rachel. She's alive. The Court has ordered you to be released immediately." Lucian grasped his father's arms. "You're free."

"What?" Zachariah's mouth fell open.

"Rachel is in custody. She's not dead. Your conviction has been overturned." Lucian said, grinning.

"I hope you know that I was just doing my job," Judd said, touching Zachariah's arm and squeezing it. "I sincerely believed she was dead and that you'd killed her. I had no idea of the treachery that woman must have been up to – disappearing and letting everyone think you'd killed her."

Zachariah's face turned ashen.

"Rachel is here?"

"Yes, dad. She's alive."

"What about her daughter? Where is she?" Zachariah said, his voice urgent.

"Her daughter? How did you know she had a daugh..." Lucian said.

"Where is she?" Zachariah's voice thundered.

"She's at large, but the Descendants have their best men out looking for her. It's just a matter of time before they bring her in as well."

Zachariah stared at him, his face aging before Lucian's eyes, as though each second added another year. He now looked like the old man that he was.

"Dad?"

"Oh no, son. No, no, no." Zachariah sank to the floor. "You've ruined everything."

CHAPTER THIRTY-THREE

MALINGER:
TO PRETEND ILLNESS

I came to in familiar surroundings. Rubbing my eyes, I peered at the walls. Yes, this was the exact same cell I'd been in this morning. It seemed like a million years ago.

Raspy sat on a stool in the corner. I scrambled to my feet and he jumped up.

"Don't try nothin'," he said. He held up his hands as though warding me off, looked down at them as though they belonged to someone else, and dropped them to his sides. His face went pink.

What the heck was I going to try?

"Golgoran will be here any minute, so just stay over there on your side until he gets here. The door is locked from the outside so you can't get out." The uncomfortable look on his face said, "And neither can I."

My mind raced. I had to get out of here. I couldn't count on some mysterious stranger to rescue me this time.

What was I going to do? Even if I somehow got past Raspy and figured out how to open the locked door, then I'd have the whole rest of the Enemy cabal to get past. Totally impossible.

I started feeling lightheaded. Uh oh. I was breathing too fast. Crap! Now was not the time to have a panic attack. I tried to get control of my breathing. Slow breath in, hold, slow breath out. But then, a seed of an idea planted in my head.

Maybe a panic attack was just what I needed right now.

I quit trying to control my breathing. I helped it along, breathing quickly and shallowly, making sure I never took in a deep breath of air. I groaned and fell to the floor. Okay, I really didn't feel that bad yet but hey, I figured some dramatics were called for.

"Don't you try nothin'," Raspy said. "Get up."

I kept breathing rapidly. It wasn't hard. Panic was bubbling in my veins – I just gave into it. I thought of every horrible thing that could happen to me if I couldn't get out of here. Golgoran would interrogate me, staring at me with those bottomless eyes. He might try cutting off my hand and taping the Piece of Home to it. After all, I'd still be alive, just missing one hand, so if it didn't work, he'd still have me in reserve to hold the Piece of Home. My arms started to tingle.

"You don't fool me," Raspy said. "Knock it off."

I allowed my thoughts to continue to spiral out of control. Golgoran would make me do whatever he needed me to do to get back into heaven. After what I'd just seen on the battle field, I had no doubt that the Enemy did outnumber the Good Guys. Maybe they didn't outnumber the angels in heaven, but I totally believed they had swarms of soldiers, like an endless sea of army ants, waiting to re-fight the battle for heaven. My arms throbbed, and my hands started to curl.

And what about my parents? What would happen to them? And

my brothers? I groaned. The pain was real now, excruciating. I curled into a fetal position, my fingers now curling into stiff claws.

"What's happening?" Raspy ran over to me. I looked at him mutely. I couldn't have said anything if I'd wanted to.

"Crap." Raspy grabbed my fingers, trying in vain to uncurl them. "Don't you die on me. Golgoran will kill me if you die on me."

He ran to the door and pounded on it. "Open up. We got an emergency in here."

"You know I can't do that until Golgoran gets here," said a muffled voice.

"You better open this door right now. She's dyin' in here."

"What's wrong with her?" the voice said.

"I don't know! She's lyin' on the floor, her hands are all curled up, her face is whiter than a piece of paper, and she's breathin' like she just ran a sprint. Get in here!"

"I don't know," the voice said. "We could get in big trouble."

"We're going to be in big trouble if she dies," Raspy yelled, kicking the door. "Move it."

Keys rattled on the other side and the door swung open a few seconds later. Footsteps rushed towards me. My hands and arms felt like someone was having a field day with a taser using me as target practice. My feet started to curl within my boots. I couldn't focus on the faces peering at me.

"Oh no. What did you do to her?"

"Nothing," Raspy squeaked. "It just happened."

"Let's get her to the infirmary, quick. You take her. I'll call ahead."

I felt myself lifted from the ground and then Raspy started running. I bounced up and down, jostling against his chest. Moments later, I felt myself plunked down on something that felt like a mattress.

"I don't know what happened," I heard Raspy say. "She just fell to the floor and her hands started curling up like that."

Warm hands grasped mine, feeling the rigid fingers. Fingers pressed against my wrist, holding for a moment, as though checking my pulse. A hand was pressed to my forehead, as though checking my temperature.

"Well," Raspy said. "Is she dying?"

"I don't know," a crisp voice said in a snotty tone. "My medical specialty relates to angels and their progeny. I don't know why you drug this human in here." He said the word 'human' in the same tone of voice you'd use if saying 'this one-celled amoeba'.

"But you gotta do something," Raspy said.

"I don't know what you expect me to do," Dr. Snotty said, sounding uninterested. "She'll either get better or she won't."

"Do you know who this is? If she doesn't get better, we're in big trouble."

"Not me, just you." Footsteps moved away from me.

"This is Ariel. You know, the girl that has the Piece of Home? If you can't fix her, Golgoran will not be happy."

The footsteps stopped. "This – this is the girl?" Dr. Snotty now sounded a bit less assured.

"Yes. Do something." Raspy's voice was loud.

I could barely concentrate on the voices. The nerves in my lower arms and legs vibrated like they'd been plugged into an electrical outlet. My hands and feet ached, contorted into shapes mimicking a 105-year-old with severe rheumatoid arthritis. I curled into a fetal position, unable to stop the moans from coming from my mouth. I felt feral, not caring what I looked like or how I sounded. Nothing existed but me and the pain.

"Did she eat something? Drink something?"

"Not since we've had her," Raspy said. "But I got no idea what she did before. Could she be on drugs? Or she's been drinkin'?"

"How should I know?" Dr. Snotty now sounded downright panicked.

"Well, I gotta go tell Gol – "

"Don't you dare tell him you idiot. Do you want to get us both killed?"

"Hey, who you callin' an idiot? I'm not the one who can't do their job. My job was to get her. I did. I got nothing to do with whatever this is."

"Well, I don't either. But do you think Golgoran cares about that?"

There was a silence.

"It's best for both of us to keep this quiet until we can get a handle on this thing."

"Golgoran was comin' to interrogate her at any moment when I brought her up here. I gotta tell him somethin'."

"Okay, okay." Footsteps paced by my bed.

"Can't you do something? She looks like she's dyin'."

At that moment, I wanted to die. It had all seemed so logical when I was planning this in the cell. I'd purposely hyperventilate until I went into hypocalcemia, and then I'd just breathe in deeply, hold for a second, and let it out like the nurse had described and this would all stop.

Slight glitch. It wasn't working. I couldn't make it stop. I rolled, groaning, wanting the discomfort to end. Sweat poured off of me. I breathed in, held it, breathed out. Nothing.

I tried again, and again. I couldn't think. I couldn't breathe. Maybe I was actually dying.

And then I passed out.

CHAPTER THIRTY-FOUR

Gambit:
Any maneuver by which one seeks to gain an advantage

"She's coming to," I heard Dr. Snotty say. "I think she's getting better. Her color is coming back."

I kept my eyes closed, mentally checking my status. The electric currents in my arms had died to just a faint numbness. My hands were no longer rigid. A wave of relief rolled over me.

Wait. No. The whole point of this was for them to think I was deathly ill. I contorted my hands and curled up into a fetal position. At the same time, I concentrated on a glacial breathing rhythm, trying to picture all the calcium or whatever the nurse had said jumped ship in my cells scurrying back to their normal places. My head cleared, and the dizziness receded, but I did my best to look like things were getting worse.

"Oh no. There she goes again." Dr. Snotty sounded panicked.

"I gotta go tell Golgoran," Raspy said, his voice shaking. "I just hope he lets me die quick."

"Hold on a minute, just hold on." Footsteps paced back and forth near my ears. "Okay, here's what we'll do. You go tell Golgoran that she had a dizzy spell and she's in the infirmary with me. Head him off as long as you can. I'll try to figure this out." Dr. Snotty said.

"I'm not gonna be able to hold him off for long," Raspy said.

"Tell him she's throwing up all over the place. That should keep him away for a while."

"Okay." Raspy's voice sounded dubious. "But he's used to seeing pretty gory stuff."

"Use the words 'projectile vomiting'."

"Projecta-what?"

"Projectile..." I heard a sigh. "Tell him vomit is shooting straight out of her mouth like Linda Blair in *The Exorcist*."

"Who...in what?"

I heard a long sigh and a muttered, "I can't believe I have to work with these Neanderthals." Then, "Tell him she's vomiting like that blonde girl in *Pitch Perfect*."

"Oh, got it. The boss loved *Pitch Perfect*. Yeah, that should keep him away."

I heard typing on a keyboard. "Contorted hands, fetal position, ashen face..." Dr. Snotty's voice was low, as though talking to himself.

I was running out of time. Dr. Snotty would figure out what was going on with me soon and then I'd lose my chance. Why didn't Raspy leave?

As if reading my mind, the typing stopped. "Why are you still here? Go, before someone comes looking for her. I don't want Golgoran anywhere near here."

"Right." I heard steps and then a door opening and closing. The typing and muttering resumed.

Yes! I was feeling almost normal. A little woozy, but still pretty good. It was time to put the second part of my plan into effect.

I don't know why I'd never thought of this before. It had come to me out of desperation in that dank little cell. I wasn't a mere harmless, height-challenged, defenseless human. Okay, I was, but I had one thing they didn't have. A gift for hyper-ventilation, and, apparently, for calcium depletion.

I opened my eyes and gingerly got to my feet. Everything worked. Fingers and toes stayed straight, my legs held me effortlessly, my arms didn't even have the faintest tingle. I saw a man standing with his back to me against the opposite wall. From the back, he looked kind of schlubby, and couldn't have been more than a couple of inches taller than me. He didn't match the voice I'd heard at all. He bent over a keyboard on a standup desk, reading the screen.

"Could it be as simple as a panic attack?" I heard Dr. Snotty mutter.

Not quite, but he was getting closer.

I kept moving toward the door. I put my hand out, grasped the handle and began to pull it down, going slowly so that it wouldn't make any noise.

It squeaked.

Dr. Snotty turned and we both jumped.

I wrenched the door open but my second's delay cost me. His hand grabbed my arm.

I yanked, but his grip didn't loosen. I stomped on his foot as hard as I could with my boot. He dropped my arm and I leapt to the hallway. An arm grabbed me around the waist, whirling me back to face him. His face was red and sweaty. I strained away from him, as much to avoid his sweat dropping on me as to get away.

"Get back here," he said, panting. The guy really needed to spend a bit more time in the gym. If I could just break his grip, I was pretty sure I could outrun him. But the sheer weight of his arm backed by the extra flab on his frame held me in place. I twisted, pulling as far away from him as far as possible, pushing against his chest with both arms, but he held on, using his free hand to try to grab my flailing arms.

The ex-cop that had run the self-defense class had warned all of us that stand and fight was not a good strategy. I felt like Rocky trapped in the corner of the boxing ring with his trainer screaming "get out of there".

I kneed him viciously in the groin. Nothing. He didn't even wince.

Did I miss? Did he not have the right, er, equipment? No time to figure it out now. I was in big trouble.

The instructor had drilled into our cream puff heads (yes, he called us cream puffs) the importance of catching our assailant off guard. He'd made a special point of doing that with me, since most of the traditional tactics didn't work at my size. It's hard to break someone's nose with the top of your head when your eye level is barely north of the average person's navel. Kicking someone's feet out from under them looks cool, but when you're outweighed by a hundred plus pounds, the odds of that are somewhere below ten percent.

"Use your head, shrimp," he'd said. "You're smart enough. Distract, dazzle, confuse, lie, cheat – do whatever you can to get away. Tactics. That's what's going to work for you."

I could probably try to break Dr. Snotty's nose, but I'd never tried that before. What part of my head should I use? Could I get high enough? What if I broke my own nose? No, I'd have to do something else.

Bile rose in the back of my throat as the idea came to me. I swallowed hard, gagging the bile down.

Ugh. Here goes.

I stopped struggling, and looked up at him, shuddering as a bead of sweat from his upper lip hit my forehead.

Startled at my sudden acquiescence, he looked down at me. I stood on my tiptoes and planted a kiss on his chubby mouth, pressing my lips to his firmly. When he gasped, his lips opened, and I brought my hands to his face, deepening the kiss. His arms loosened and I twisted away, sprinting down the hall as fast as I could.

I heard his steps clomping behind me, but, as I'd suspected, he couldn't keep up, and after a few seconds I didn't hear them at all. I fled around a corner and stopped, wiping my mouth, and yes, even my tongue, with the back of my sleeve. Yech.

Okay, I was free inside the Enemy's Headquarters, an anthill of a place with probably thousands of soldiers who'd all be on red alert in minutes looking for me.

Now what?

CHAPTER THIRTY-FIVE

Digerati:
Tech nerds

raced down the corridor, heart pounding. The good news was that the first part of my plan had worked – getting out of that dank cell. The bad news? I had no clue as to how to get out of this place.

I didn't even know if we were above ground, below ground, or – wait – were we even attached to the ground? I'd been transported to the place both times today so I had no idea where we were. For all I knew, we could be in Cincinnati, although that seemed like it might be a bit inconvenient.

I skidded around a corner and saw a long hall ahead of me that looked vaguely familiar. Yes, this was the other end of the corridor I'd been hauled down by Raspy and the gang after leaving Golgoran's office earlier today. I couldn't go that way. I should have turned right and not left when I ran out of the infirmary.

I turned to head back but then heard footsteps pounding down the hallway punctuated by the type of harsh panting you'd expect from a three pack a day smoker only days away from a permanent tracheotomy. Dr. Snotty. Seriously, the guy's totally pharisaical, preaching one thing and doing another. You'd think that someone who chose to be a doctor would take better care of himself.

I had no choice but to keep going down the hallway. Wheezebag or not, I didn't think I could get by him. All he'd have to do was fall on me and I'd be toast. I took off again, but then slowed as I neared an open doorway. An odd humming sound came from the room. I slowed, then tiptoed up to the doorframe. I counted to three, and then peeked around the corner into the room.

Computer monitors and televisions glowed against the dim lighting in the cavernous room. A giant piece of complicated looking equipment held down one entire wall, pulsing with tiny red, yellow and green lights. It was the room I'd seen earlier in the day, the one that looked like a huge electronic control center.

Heavy footsteps echoed behind me. It would only be a matter of seconds before Dr. Snotty turned the corner and saw me.

Two people wearing headphones sat in the control room, both glued to their computer screens. Before I could second guess myself, I eased into the room, dropping quietly to the floor. I tensed, waiting for one of the them to say "what are you doing in here," or something like that.

Nothing happened. I let out the breath I hadn't known I'd been holding. It was then I noticed that there were actually two floor levels in the room. All the desks with their computers were on a raised platform a little under two feet high. The platform began about five feet into the room and then covered the rest of the floor. A whirring sound came from it, and cool air wafted from underneath, strong enough to ruffle my hair. I'd seen something like this before, although not nearly as big. A cooling floor kept all the electronic equipment from overheating.

Dr. Snotty's footsteps got closer and I cringed. What would I do if he looked into the room?

The footsteps slowed and then stopped. All I could hear now was his panting.

Why had he stopped?

"Dr. McGregor," a voice echoed down the hall way outside. I didn't think my heart could beat any faster, but I'd been wrong. I knew that voice.

"Why aren't you with your patient?"

Golgoran. My skin crawled.

"She – " The panting morphed into a whistling gasp.

I scooted farther into the room, around the corner of the platform.

"Get hold of yourself. Did you leave her alone?"

"No," the doctor said, the word coming out on a wheeze.

Okay, big trouble. Sooner or later the doctor would spill the beans and they'd know that not only had I escaped, but that I was probably somewhere on this hallway since Golgoran had been at one end and the doctor had been pounding down the other. My eyes darted around the room but I couldn't see much because I was on the floor and my vision was blocked by the platform.

"He pro-ly needs a second to catch his breath," I heard Raspy say.

"I don't want to hear another syllable from you, you imbecile. You should have called me the second she became ill," Golgoran said.

"I told you boss. I didn't have time – I thought she was dyin'." Raspy's voice rose so high he almost sounded like Squeaky.

Something caught my eye. The platform was made up of thin, white tiles held in place in metal grids. I raised my head slightly, examining the tiles. As my eyes adjusted to the dimness, I noticed a round hole in the floor of the platform closest to me. A fat bundle of wires snaked from something that I couldn't see down through the hole and underneath the platform. I raised my head a bit further, and saw similar holes and bundles of wires and cords dotting the platform's floor across its width, all leading under the platform.

"I told you, not another – " and then Golgoran's voice changed, sounding panicked. "Is she dead?"

The platform was hollow underneath. All the electrical plugs and wires were attached somewhere underneath to a power source.

The doctor must have shaken his head "no", because then I heard Golgoran say, "Well, then where is she? Speak up."

I pushed on one of the tiles on the side of the platform. It didn't move.

"I'm," gasp, "trying."

I wouldn't want to be Dr. Snotty right now.

"Try harder."

"She ran," the doctor said.

"What? You let her get away?"

"She," cough, "tricked me."

"How?"

"She - "

"Never mind. We'll deal with that later. Where did she go?"

Uh oh. Time was just about out. I pushed harder on the tile. Still nothing. There had to be a way to get under the platform. My fingers traced the metal grid holding the tile in place.

"She ran down...this...hall."

"Which way?"

"Towards you."

Footsteps entered the control room. I shrank against the platform, thankful that I had backed around the corner.

"Have you seen anyone come in here?" Golgoran said.

Nothing.

"Hey," he shouted, loud enough that I jumped.

I heard a chair fall over and feet moving.

"Sir?" a voice said.

"I said, have you seen anyone come in here?"

"No, sir," two voices said, almost simultaneously.

Footsteps retreated. "We need to look in the other rooms on this hallway," Golgoran said, his voice fading.

"What was that about?" I heard one of the nerds say.

"I don't know, but he scared the crap out of me," another voice said. "Part of the reason I took this job is because he hates technology so much he never comes down here."

I didn't have much time. I knew they'd be back. I examined the metal around the tile and saw that it had screws holding it in place. I eased my backpack off my shoulders and unzipped it slowly, trying to not to make any noise. Thankfully, the hum of the computers, the muted chatter on the televisions and the whirr of the air-conditioned platform drowned out the sound.

I felt along the bottom of the backpack for coins, berating myself for my sloppy habit of throwing my change into my pack instead of putting them into the coin purse area of my wallet. I hadn't ever thought of it as a life-threatening practice until now.

My fingers found a coin and I fished out a quarter. I tried to insert it into the head of the screw, but it was too big.

I dug in my backpack again, finding a penny this time. I didn't have much hope that it would fit, but I tried it anyway. No luck.

I felt along the bottom of the pack again. I needed a dime. I felt various coins, but none were thin enough to be a dime.

I examined my thumbnail, the longest nail I had, and tried it in the groove of the screwhead. The nail ripped. I sucked in a breath, holding in a small scream. Man, that hurt.

"She's got to be in the control room." Golgoran's voice filtered down the hallway, moving closer. My hands started to sweat.

I turned the back pack almost upside down, holding onto the logbook and other articles and letting the smaller objects slide to the opening. Yes! I grabbed the dime and tried it on the screw. It turned. I unscrewed it all the way, placing the screw on the floor and moving on to the next one.

"How do we get some lights on in here?" Golgoran said from the doorway. I dropped the dime and for a heart-stopping second thought I'd lost it. I almost fainted with relief when my fingers found it, and I went back to work on the second screw.

"S-sir?" I heard one of the nerds say.

"Take those ridiculous earphones off," Golgoran snapped.

"Yes sir."

"I said, how do we turn the lights on in here?"

The second screw fell to the floor and I scrambled over to the screws on the other end of the tile. Two down, two to go.

"The light switch is behind you, sir."

My hands shook so much I had to use both hands to guide the dime into the third screw.

I heard the click of a switch and the room was flooded with fluorescent light. It wouldn't be long before they'd find me. I pressed the dime into the groove and turned as fast as I could. The screw fell to the floor. The only thing holding the tile in place was the screw at the top rightmost corner.

"Spread out and look everywhere – under every desk, behind every cabinet, in any conceivable hiding place."

I heard shoes stepping onto the platform, and seconds later footsteps headed my way. I had run out of time. I pushed the tile up, the top screw holding the one corner in place and wriggled through the opening headfirst, dragging my backpack after me. I twisted toward the tile, pulling the edge of it back down toward the floor.

The tap of footsteps echoed in my ears, coming to a stop directly over my head.

I held my breath. Whoever it was seemed to stand there forever. Then the footsteps retreated back the way they'd came.

I let my breath out slowly, dizzy with relief. I heard sounds of moving furniture, desk legs scraping on the platform floor, the sound of rollers under heavy equipment stands squeaking past above my head.

"Where is she?" Golgoran thundered.

"I d-don't know," one of the nerds said in a whisper.

"I wasn't talking to you," he growled. "It's obvious that you know nothing."

"Maybe she got past us boss," Raspy said.

"Is she invisible?"

"No."

"Can she transport?"

"No."

"Can she shrink herself like Ant Man?"

"No, boss."

"Then she's here." Footsteps paced slowly back and forth above my head. There was a tap on the floor.

"What's under this?"

"J-just plugs and cords. It's a c-cooled floor for our equipment," I heard one of the nerds say.

"Are these tiles removable?"

My stomach rolled. What if they pulled up the tiles? I began crawling backwards.

"Yes."

Someone stepped off the platform. I didn't hear anything for a second, and then the footsteps began walking toward my end of the platform. I heard a pecking noise. What was that? And then it hit me.

The person was tapping on each tile on the side of the platform.

I fought back nausea.

The tapping came closer. I inched away from the tapping, my heart pounding.

Tap tap. Step. Tap tap. Step. Tap tap. Step. Tap...

There was a rattling sound. The one screw holding the tile in front of me in place wasn't enough to keep the tile from banging against the metal grid.

I scuttled backwards, and then turned myself totally around and crawled as fast as I could away from the tile.

"She's under the platform," Golgoran said, his voice ringing with excitement.

I banged into cords, pulling them free in my mad dash away from the loose tile.

"Get over here." I heard a sliding sound as the tile was lifted up to reveal the opening through which I'd crawled. "Go in after her!"

"Beep, beep beep," I heard as a mechanical alarm went off.

"Wait," one of the nerds said. "She's pulling out the cords. Our electric connections are under there. It'll crash the system if you just bulldoze under there."

"She's already bulldozed in there. Go after her," Golgoran said.

"I can't fit under there," Raspy said.

"Get in there," Golgoran yelled.

Which way should I go? Where was there to go? All I'd seen was a room with a raised platform which extended to the back of the room. My mind raced. Three sides of the platform led straight back out into the room; i.e. straight into Golgoran. The back of the room led to – well, a wall.

I was trapped.

"See? I can't even get my shoulders in there," Raspy said.

"Tear up the floor. Now." Golgoran said.

If I remembered right, the heavy equipment was at the back of the room, against the wall. If I went there, at least it would take them longer to get to me.

Right. That would just give me extra moments of terror to contemplate what lay ahead of me. Still, I headed to the back of the room. I didn't know what else to do. I tore at the cords in my way. More alarms blared, and my ears rang.

"Stop, stop," I heard one of the nerds cry, barely audible over the alarms. "We're going to lose everything. Our entire grid will be exposed."

Good. I didn't know what that meant, but if it was bad for the Enemy, it had to be good for me. I kept going, propelling myself under the platform like a swimmer, going in the direction of the back wall, pulling out every cord I ran into on the way. My hand hit the wall seconds later and I pulled up.

What was that?

The lower two feet of the wall, the part covered by the platform, consisted of a series of rectangular box fans, all slowing to a stop. I must have unplugged whatever was powering them.

I smelled the familiar scent of pine and firewood and felt a slight breeze. I touched the fans, and then figured it out. The fans were used to draw the outside air in to cool the floor. Why have a fancy air conditioning system when you could just use the frigid air from outside?

A terrific crash sounded in the direction from which I'd come.

"Aargh!" Raspy cried.

"You can't break the tiles," the talking nerd said. "They can withstand hundreds of pounds of pressure. They have to be to hold all of this equipment."

"Wish you woulda tol' me that before I broke my hand," Raspy's voice growled.

"You didn't give me time –"

"Shut up," Golgoran said. "Get an axe or a welding torch or whatever you need to get through these tiles. Now."

"They're held in place by screws. We just have to take them out of a few of the tiles and then we can get to her," one of the nerds said.

"We don't have time for that," Golgoran said. "I don't care how you do it. Tear these tiles up now."

"Please sir," the tech nerd said, his voice pitched an octave higher than it had been. "This is a delicate environment."

"She's not goin' anywhere, boss," Raspy said. "She's stuck under there like a cockroach under a refrigerator."

I heard a click and then saw a glow coming through the tiles. A long, thin glow. My stomach dropped. I knew what that was. A light sword.

The tiles crackled as the glow bore down on one of the tiles close to where I'd crawled under the platform. Then a horrible stench filled my nose, like rotting chemicals being boiled.

"It's not cutting through," Raspy said.

"But it's bending it. This will trap her in there until we can get the screws out," Golgoran said.

I peered in the direction of the glow. My breath quickened. A tile had sunk down towards the floor like the bottom end of a bowl, hanging from the metal frame, cutting off any chance of exiting the way I'd come. As I watched, another tile melted away from the sword, bowing to the floor.

The glowing tip of the light sword moved closer, scorching another tile, and then another. Sooner or later he'd pick one close to me and figure out where I was.

I looked back at the wall of fans. I tried to see what held them in place, but it was too dark.

I pushed on one of them with my hands. It didn't move. I scooted over, testing each fan. The second one to the right gave just a hair. It was my best bet.

I glanced behind me. A dozen bubbles of melted tile sagged to the floor around me. I braced myself and raised my feet as high as the space would allow. One, two three...

I couldn't do it. My plan was to kick the fan as hard as I could, hoping to knock it out of its frame and crawl to the outside. But, if I kicked, Golgoran would hear me. He'd know exactly where I was.

Maybe if I just waited, I'd come up with a better idea. Or they'd decide I wasn't under the floor after all, and I could find a chance to get out when no one was in the room and wouldn't be able to hear me kick at the fan. Or...

The tile inches from my face smoldered and began sagging to the floor. I jerked out of the way, gagging on the odor.

Then the tile by my feet started its stretch downward. If I didn't break out of here now, I'd be cut off from the fans.

I sucked in a breath, struggling between wanting to throw up and wanting to pass out. I raised my feet, closed my eyes, and struck the fan with both feet as hard as I could. It budged a bit, but didn't break loose.

"Did you hear that?" Golgoran said. "She's right here."

I kicked again at the fan. Footsteps pounded over to where I was. I envisioned Raspy, the two nerds, Golgoran, and Dr. Snotty all standing over me. The thought galvanized me. I kicked furiously at the fan.

"She's gotta be right here. Get 'er boss," Raspy said.

The tile over my head began to smoke. I scrunched forward, repositioning myself with my back to the fans.

"What's she doin'?" Raspy said.

"I don't know. But we've got her now," Golgoran said.

I dug my feet in and pushed as hard as I could with my back. Nothing. This wasn't going to work. I jackknifed, reversing to put my hands by the loose fan. I beat on it. Ow! My fists throbbed.

I thought when you were buzzing with adrenaline and fighting for your life, you didn't feel pain. Nobody seemed to feel it in the movies. People were shot and knifed, and beaten so hard that eight or nine ribs had to be broken, and still they ran for miles after the bad guy and got their man, not succumbing to their injuries until after the excitement was all over.

That wasn't happening. Even with my life at stake, I couldn't bring myself to hit the fan again with my fists. What a wimp.

"Do that tile," Raspy said, and a second later the tile at my feet bubbled. I drew my feet up. I was just inches away from being in a total fetal position.

I scrabbled for my backpack. Using it to protect my hands. I pounded it against the fan as hard as I could.

One corner gave.

Heat radiated right over my head, and I knew the tile was seconds away from sagging onto my scalp. I twisted but I couldn't move out of the way. The other tile bubbles had me trapped. My whole body shook. My scalp would be burned to a crisp, or maybe my skull would be crushed or the tile would ooze over my whole head, burning me while suffocating me so I'd die in excruciating, unfathomable pain or...

"Do you want to kill me?" I yelled. Had I just said that? Yes, I had.

The heat retreated but I could still see the red glow through the tile above my head.

"You don't wanna do that boss," Raspy said. "We need her – AARGH!"

And then I heard a thump above me.

"I would like you to shut up," Golgoran said.

"You just cut his arm off," I heard Dr. Snotty say.

"It'll grow back," Golgoran said in a dismissive tone. "I –"

But I'd quit listening. I hit the fan again, putting as much force as I could behind my backpack-protected hands.

It gave.

I scrabbled through the hole, breathing in the snowy air.

I was out.

CHAPTER THIRTY-SIX

OUT-HEROD:
TO EXCEED IN CRUELTY OR VIOLENCE

I looked around. I'd emerged into what looked like a wreck of a barn. Rotting boards hung together in a semblance of outer walls, and one whole side was missing. I ran out the missing side and looked back. Anyone coming by would just see an ancient abandoned barn. The Enemy's headquarters must all be underneath. How appropriate.

I hitched my backpack onto my shoulders and looked around. Where was I?

I saw no roads, no street lights, no distant city lights, but I smelled a distant odor of firewood. I took a few steps away from the barn, hoping to see something, anything.

Nothing.

The cold ate through my clothes. Somewhere along the way, I'd lost my coat. The Enemy would figure out soon that I'd escaped to the outside and come after me. I turned in a slow circle, trying to see anything that would give me some idea of which way to go. If by some miracle the Enemy didn't catch me wandering around like the directionless wingnut that I am, I'd freeze to death.

I had my phone. I could call someone.

I dug it out and then stopped. Who to call? I ticked them off in my mind. There was Michael, who thought I was some kind of Mata Hari; my parents, who were prisoners of the Descendants; Lucian, who apparently thought I was something close to the devil incarnate; Barnaby, who thought I'd joined the Enemy; Todd, who thought I'd killed Samantha...

Tears burned at the back of my eyes. Samantha.

I shook my head. No time to think of that now. At least the phone had a GPS on it. I tapped the phone.

Nothing.

I hit the power button and held it.

Nothing.

The phone was dead.

"I can't believe you actually got out, Weeny," a voice said from behind me.

I whirled.

"Rosamund?"

And then my breath stopped.

"Aaron?"

My less than stellar bodyguard and her murdering ex-fiance stood before me like deadly Ken and Barbie dolls come to life.

CHAPTER THIRTY-SEVEN

CLIMACTERIC: HAVING EXTREME OR FAR REACHING IMPLICATIONS

wanted to run but my feet wouldn't move.

Aaron held his hands up, palms facing me. "We're not here to hurt you."

"You look like you're about to pass out," Rosamund said. I could tell she was trying to sound sympathetic, but it came out as snarky. She was enjoying this, that witch. Aaron shot her a reproving look.

White spots flickered in front of my eyes. I'd like to fall into the oblivion of unconsciousness, but then where would I wake up? Or would I wake up at all?

I sucked in a deep breath of air and took a step back.

"We're here to help," Aaron said,

I giggled. An old joke my dad loved flitted across my brain. What are the nine scariest words ever said? "We're from the government and we're here to help".

"I think she's losing it," Rosamund said.

Aaron took a step toward me. I snapped out of my stupor. Fumbling at my neck, I jerked on the Piece of Home, breaking the strap I'd tied around it to fashion a pseudo necklace.

"Stay back," I said, holding the Piece of Home in front of me like a talisman.

"Whoa," Aaron said. Rosamund's eyes widened, and for once she kept her mouth shut.

"Don't take another step. You know what this can do." I waved the Piece of Home at them.

I don't know why I hadn't thought of this before. All this time, I'd had a weapon. It wouldn't kill, but the pain of a burn would at least slow them down. Wait, maybe it would kill. If I burned through their necks, using the Piece of Home as a kind of deadly heated laser, decapitating them, that would do it.

I fought back a gag. Definitely NOT going to do that.

"Now you're going to back up to the road over there," I gestured to the street twenty yards away, "and then I'm going to leave, and you're not going to follow me."

"Weeny, you're really bad at this." Rosamund snorted. "We can just transport and land in front of you."

"Rosamund, would you please just shut up?" Aaron's voice was mild, but Rosamund's face reddened.

"I was just trying to help," she muttered, shrugging.

"Just listen to me, Ariel," Aaron said. "We're on the same side. "

Now it was my turn to snort.

"We don't have much time," Aaron said, speaking quickly. "They're going to figure out pretty soon that you got out, and even that," he gestured toward the Piece of Home, "won't help you with a horde of the Enemy. They'll be too many for you to overcome them all."

"You murdered your parents. You almost killed Dr. Fielding. You were trying to get Golgoran to give me to you to get the Piece of Home away. You talked about," I gulped, "cutting my hand off. You killed cats." The cat thing really wasn't relevant, but it was so horrible that I couldn't help blurting it out.

Aaron groaned and shook his head. "I didn't do any of those things. And I kept you from getting your hand cut off, if you remember. I can explain everything. But we have to go, now."

"But I saw you. At Dr. Fielding's. You almost killed him, and then you threatened me," I said, my voice rising.

"I came just in time to prevent Achimalech's thugs from killing Dr. Fielding. And I threatened you to try to get the Piece of Home away from you before you handed it over to Michael, which would have put it straight into Achimalech's hands." He blew out a breath. "We don't have time for this."

"What about the cats?"

He blew out a breath. "Really? That's what you want to talk about now?"

I stared back at him.

"Okay, okay. I didn't kill any cats. That was done to make me look bad."

"Why should I believe you?" This was all happening too fast. How could I make a decision like this in a split second?

"Look." Aaron held out his hands. "Let me transport you away from here, and then I'll tell you everything. And you'll still have the Piece of Home and you can burn the crap out of me if you want."

On its face, that idea might have worked, but he could transport me right back inside the Enemy's Headquarters to a horde of Bad Guys waiting to overpower me just like he'd said. I wasn't falling for that trick.

"Get away from me." I took a step back.

"Where are you going to go?" Aaron said. "You've got to have help, and right now we're all you've got. The Descendants think you're with the Enemy. Your parents are prisoners, Barnaby is on lockdown –"

"He is?"

"Yeah, they're afraid he'll help you."

I felt a rush of warmth. At least Barnaby hadn't abandoned me. As for Michael and Lucian...the warmth evaporated.

"We're your only hope," Aaron said.

My mind reeled. All I had were bad choices. Aaron was right. I needed help. But these two?

Aaron shook his head impatiently.

"Who do you think got you out of your cell earlier today?"

"That was you?" I said.

He nodded.

That could just be a lie. The Enemy knew someone had helped me escape.

"How do I know that was you? I never saw whoever transported me out of there, and their voice was modified."

"You know because I told you that you couldn't trust anyone," he said. "And you asked me if that included Michael and I said yes."

I rocked back on my heels. How could he know that unless he'd been the one who'd rescued me? But before I could say anything, Rosamund stepped toward me, looking like a pressure cooker about to pop.

"We're risking out lives standing out here waiting for you, you midget," she said.

Aaron put a restraining hand on her arm. She shook him off. "No, I won't shut up. The world has been revolving around her since she came to Bozeman, with everyone hopping around like she's something special – Michael, Barnaby, Lucian, Daniel – even Cyrus, for goodness sakes! The only thing special about her is that she has the Piece of Home. Now she's going to get us all killed because she's too stupid to know how to protect it. And......wait. What is it?"

She must have read my face, which had dropped the second she said his name.

"Cyrus is dead," I said, my voice shaking.

"What?" Rosamund's face paled.

"How?" Aaron's face tightened.

"The Enemy killed him."

Rosamund's eyes flooded with tears and Aaron put an arm around her. She buried her head in his chest and he held her, his face grim. After a moment, he released her and looked back at me.

"We're out of time. They'll figure out where you are any second," he said. His face was stoic but his eyes were bleak.

I looked at the two of them. Either they were Oscar-worthy actors, or they were truly devastated over Cyrus' death. I made my decision.

"Okay, okay," I said slowly. "I'll go with you." I stepped over to Aaron, my heart thumping so hard I thought I might have a heart attack.

"Let's go," he said putting his arms around me. I felt my cells begin to loosen as we prepared to transport.

In a few seconds I'd know if I'd made the biggest – and last – mistake of my life.

CHAPTER THIRTY-EIGHT

CHICANERY: THE USE OF TRICKERY TO ACHIEVE A FINANCIAL, LEGAL OR POLITICAL RESULT

Six Years Ago

The pink chiffon top his mother had worn to the state dinner given for the visiting South American Descendants had a wide,bloody hole in the front. She lay on her back on the floor, her eyes frozen open with a look somewhere between horror and surprise.

Her hand reached out toward his father, lying three feet away. Aaron gagged. His father's head lay to the side of his body, his eyes mercifully shut.

Aaron ran to the bodies. What had happened? Where were the guards? Had someone staged a coup? He'd heard rumblings, but assumed that it was the idle gossip his father had insisted it was.

"Aaron, thank goodness." The door burst open and Achimalech

rushed into the room, followed by five armored guards. "I was afraid they had taken you, or worse, killed you like they did your parents." He hugged Aaron to him, turning him away so he could no longer see his parents' gruesome corpses.

"Who killed them?" Aaron said, his voice muffled against Achimalech's shoulder. He stepped back, his face ashen. "What's going on?"

Achimalech kept his hand on Aaron's forearm. "A dissident group smuggled members in with the South American Descendants' entourage. They killed your parents and tried to kill Michael. We – "

"Is Michael okay?" Aaron clutched Achimalech's arm.

"He's fine. I have him under heavy guard. But you must come away with us now."

Aaron didn't move, trying not to look at his parents. He suddenly felt like a child, when just hours before he'd been demanding to be treated like an adult.

"We've got to get you out of here." Achimalech tugged on Aaron's arm.

"I can't leave them," Aaron said. He wiped his hand over his eyes. "I can't just leave them lying there." He couldn't have moved even if he'd wanted to. He felt cemented to the spot, as though the weight of what had happened had driven his feet into the ground.

"Aaron, look at me."

Aaron drug his eyes up to Achimalech's face.

"This isn't over. We haven't caught the assassins. They will want to kill you and Michael as your parents' heirs. They're looking for you right now. I don't know who to trust. These are my personal guards, who I know are trustworthy. They're going to get you out of here until we've caught these villains."

"But –"

"There's no time. You have to go. Now."

The urgency in Achimalech's voice finally broke through. Aaron moved his legs and was surprised to see that they worked, walking him over to Achimalech's guards.

He turned back to Achimalech. "Michael is safe? You trust the people with him?"

Achimalech nodded. "No one is going to get to him." He put his arms on Aaron's shoulders. In a soft voice he said, "I'll take care of everything. I'll send for you as soon as it's safe."

And to Aaron's everlasting shame, he had gone just like Achimalech had told him to.

Why hadn't he stayed? Why hadn't he insisted on personally tracking down his parent's killers?

Instead, he'd allowed himself to be transported away to New York City, of all places. His guards had insisted it was the perfect hiding place, full of people and enough electronics to make pin-pointing his aura almost impossible. One day had turned a week, and then three weeks and finally, a month. He received daily reports from the guards, and sometimes in person from Achimalech. A cabal of over a hundred traitors had ultimately been uprooted, with turncoats discovered in every sector of the Descendant's headquarters, from the Elder Council to the Imperial Guard all the way down to the goblins.

As each day passed, Aaron felt more and more like a coward. After all, he would be the new ruler of the Descendants. He should be there, hunting down all those responsible for his parents' deaths.

"If anything happens to you, Aaron, then everything will be thrown into chaos. Michael is too young to rule. The most important thing we can do is to keep you safe," Achimalech said on one of his frequent visits. "Patience is a virtue in a ruler. You have to learn to exercise it. Besides, this isn't a typical war. We're rooting these traitors out, one at a time. We're almost there."

Finally, six weeks into his exile, Aaron put his foot down.

"I'm going back. Today," he told Achimalech, and Achimalech, reading his face, knew that he would not be able to talk him out of it this time.

And that's when Aaron found out.

CHAPTER THIRTY-NINE

STRANGE BEDFELLOWS:
TWO OR MORE PEOPLE OR IDEAS WORKING TOGETHER IN AN UNEXPECTED WAY

"Found out what?" I said.

We sat in a log cabin somewhere in the Absaroka Mountains outside Bozeman. At least that's where Aaron said we were. The wind blew outside, while inside the wood in the fireplace burned with a comforting crackle. The furnishings were simple and homey, and I could feel my tense muscles loosening.

I'd been studying Aaron as he talked. He'd been born three years before Michael, but looked at least a decade older. Harsh lines formed the planes around his mouth and eyes, signaling that the last years hadn't been happy ones. I didn't trust Aaron yet, but the fear I'd had of him had ebbed enough that my heart beat at a normal rate.

"It was all a big set up, right from the start." Aaron said.

"What do you mean?"

"Achimalech had my parents killed. He wasn't rounding up traitors while I was gone. He was planting evidence incriminating me and telling everyone I had fled. I made it easy for him by leaving. Over those six weeks, everyone had finally come to believe I had actually killed my parents, even Michael." Aaron's voice grew husky over his brother's name.

"I knew you hadn't done it," Rosamund said. She laid her hand on his.

"You had a funny way of showing it," he said, removing his hand.

"I told you that wasn't a real engagement," she said, her face reddening.

"It sure looked real to me." His tone was acidic. "Come on, Rosamund. My own brother?" His lips curled.

"I told you we were just following the expectation that the new ruler would marry someone in my family. You don't understand, Aaron," she said, her voice rising. "Everything was a mess. Your parents were dead, you were gone, the kingdom was still trying to recover from...from..." she hesitated.

"You mean from the belief that I murdered my parents?" He glared at her.

"And we were just trying to create stability," she said, wringing her hands. "We never really loved each other. We were just trying to do the right thing for the kingdom."

"Funny," he said, cocking his head to one side. "I know you as well as anyone and I'd never use the word 'altruistic' to describe anything you do."

He had her there. I hadn't known Rosamund long, but I couldn't imagine her doing something as big a marrying someone just for the benefit of others.

"You're one to talk," Rosamund said, jumping to her feet. "When have you ever helped anyone out of the goodness of your heart?"

Aaron leapt to his feet. "What do you think I've been doing for the last six years?" he said in a quiet voice, which made the sound of his fist pounding on the wooden table even more jarring. The table shook with the blow.

"I don't know because you never contacted me," Rosamund shouted, moving right into his face. "I was your fiancée, and you just walked away without a single word."

"From what I heard, you were so heartbroken you started dating Isaac within a month, and then took up with my brother as soon as he was old enough to – "

"And I suppose you remained single and celibate for the past six years?" Rosamund arched an eyebrow. "Right."

Seriously, these two need couples counseling.

"In your zeal for helping, did you and Michael ever – " Aaron began.

"Stop!" I sprang to my feet and wedged myself between the two of them. "You guys need to work out your issues later. We don't have time for this right now."

They scowled at each other over my head.

"Sit down," I said, giving each of them a little shove.

They sat reluctantly, each giving the other the stink eye.

"Okay, let's get back on topic" I said. "How did Achimalech set you up?"

"Aaron made it pretty easy for him," Rosamund said, her tone on the wrong side of snarky.

Aaron's fists clenched, his knuckles turning white, and then he slowly uncurled them.

"She's right," he said, dropping his chin. "If I hadn't been such a jerk maybe none of this would have happened."

Rosamund's face softened and she lifted her hand toward him and then dropped it back in her lap.

"I guess you could say I was in my teenage rebellion years back then. I did the typical juvenile stuff, but always ratcheted up a notch.

I know now that Achimalech was egging me on, subtly goading me to do more and more, but at the time I was too naïve to see what was going on."

"You were only eighteen," Rosamund said. "Cut yourself a little slack. Plus, Achimalech was really good. His picture ought to be by the word 'manipulate' in the dictionary."

Aaron ignored her. "Achimalech always told me that Michael was my parents' favorite, relating to me little things they'd said, all about how great Michael was and what a fantastic ruler he would be. And then he'd hint at doubts they had about me, like he'd suggest that I do this or that activity to show my parents that I could exercise good judgment, the implication being that they didn't think I had good judgment."

He stood and walked to the other side of the room his back to us, talking as he went.

"One day when Achimalech knew I was coming, he left a book open in his office on the rules for disqualifying one heir in favor of another. He then made a big show of covering the book, and when I demanded to know why he was reading that section, he told me that he was studying up to defend me if my parents decided to make Michael the ruler instead of me, even though I was the eldest. He actually said they were discussing the matter."

My heart tugged at Aaron's words. I knew exactly how he had felt. My parents hadn't gone as far as his, but I'd certainly felt like the un-favored child, and it was a hurt that woke up and tore a hole in my gut at the most unexpected times.

Aaron turned to face us. "Achimalech undercut me in a thousand ways, always making it seem like it was coming from my parents. Maybe it was, maybe it wasn't." His mouth twisted. "Either way, it worked like a charm. I grew more and more resentful, and it came to a head the night my parents were murdered."

"You were a little out of control. Self-restraint was never your best quality," Rosamund said, but her tone was kind and she gave Aaron a rueful smile.

"What happened?" I said.

"It was the night of the state dinner for the leader of the South American Descendants," Rosamund said.

"Yes," Aaron said, walking back over to his chair and perching on its edge. "The leader of the South America Descendants was there for planning talks. When I was Michael's age, I'd never been allowed to go to events like state dinners because they were for adults only. But they insisted on having Michael attend the dinner even though he was only fourteen, and made a big show of introducing him to King Levi and his wife." His jaw clenched. "I hadn't even been introduced to them yet. By that point, all it took was Achimalech nudging me with his elbow with this pitying look on his face. Like he was saying, 'see, they're more proud of him than of you.'"

"I wondered what had happened," Rosamund said, taking his hand and squeezing it. "You looked like you'd bitten into a rotten egg when Michael came in."

Aaron had a faraway look on his face, as though replaying what had happened in his mind. I don't know if he even realized that Rosamund was holding his hand.

"So, I acted like a total jerk at the dinner. Everything my father said, I sneered at. In my mind, they thought I wasn't worthy of being the next ruler, and it became a self-fulfilling prophecy. I set out to prove it."

"Then I drank too much, and things got worse. I insulted King Levi, and my father ordered me to leave. I had to be dragged out. It was quite a scene." His face darkened. "The last time I saw my parents, I was fighting with them."

Rosamund released his hand and rubbed his back.

"Looking back, Achimalech had been priming me to blow, and probably had been priming my parents as well, by doing things like killing the cats and making it look like I'd done it. With my behavior at the dinner, I guess Achimalech thought there'd never be a better night to put his plan in motion. He killed my parents, or had them killed, got me to leave under the guise of protecting me, and then spent the next six weeks planting evidence and convincing everyone that I had done it. The fact that I was MIA was the best proof he had."

"I told them you hadn't done it, and that you'd probably been kidnapped or worse," Rosamund said. "But Achimalech was running things and he said that his men had tracked you to the Enemy's Headquarters."

Aaron seemed to feel Rosamund's hand on his back for the first time and slid away from her. Rosamund's cheeks blazed red. I don't know which was harder for her – Aaron rejecting her hand or me seeing him do it.

"Anyway," Aaron continued, "Achimalech then took advantage of Michael's age and his grief, and became the de facto ruler. I don't know if that was his plan all along, but it couldn't have worked out better for him. That is, until you came along," he said, giving me a half-smile. It was the first time I'd seen anything close to a smile on his face, and I saw the charming boy he must have been before Achimalech had used him. "You should have heard the moaning about the fact that not only had Achimalech been killed, but he'd been killed by a girl. I think half the Enemy are convinced you're some kind of super human."

"I wish," I said, wondering if it was okay to feel so pleased about being complimented on killing someone.

"I've spent the last six years climbing the ladder in the Enemy's hierarchy, trying to get in a position to sabotage them whenever possible. It's the only thing I could do. I didn't want to be one of them, but I couldn't go back to being with the Descendants."

"You must have been so lonely," Rosamund said.

Michael didn't look at her.

"So how did you two end up being together?" I said, glancing from one to the other.

"I arrived in the laundry room a minute after Golgoran's guys took you," Aaron said.

"And I had a weird feeling and went down to the laundry room to check on you," Rosamund said.

"We ran into each other - "

"And I wasn't about to leave him," Rosamund said, her chin jutting forward.

"I couldn't get rid of her," Aaron said, giving her a pointed look, "so I told her to come here and wait, and we've been trying to figure out how to rescue you without revealing ourselves."

We sat in silence for a moment.

I believed Aaron's story. It made sense in a weird way. And besides, what would be the point of him being here with me if he weren't on my side? He'd rescued me once, and he could have turned me back over to the Enemy when I emerged from their Headquarters an hour ago.

But I had to ask one question to be sure that he could be trusted.

"What do you think we should do with the Piece of Home?" I looked directly into Aaron's eyes.

"We have to destroy it," he said without hesitating.

"Absolutely," Rosamund said, nodding. "We've talked it over and that's the only way."

I looked at the two of them, my would-be allies: Aaron, a pariah from his own kind with a possible anger management issue who'd been living with the Enemy for years, and Rosamund, a back-stabbing conniver who disliked me so much she couldn't even carry off the title of 'frenemy'. Besides that, the two of them badly needed a stint on the Dr. Phil show to work out their six-year buildup of anger and resentment.

"If we don't destroy it – " Aaron began.

I held up my hands. "I don't need convincing. I totally agree."

Rosamund and Aaron smiled at each other for the first time.

"We were afraid you'd want to give it to Michael," Rosamund said.

"No," I said, the word coming out more forcefully than I'd intended.

Rosamund eyed me. "All righty then," she said.

"There's only one problem," Aaron said.

"What's that?" I said.

"I don't have any idea how to destroy it, and we've got no scientists and no lab to help us figure out how to get rid of it for good," Aaron said, rubbing his face.

"And the Descendants' best people haven't figured out how to do it, so I don't know how we're going to figure it out," said Rosamund.

"The Piece of Home has survived for millenia. The fact is, it may actually be indestructible." Aaron's voice was somber.

"Yeah," Rosamund said. "We may be trying to do the impossible."

Okay, so my new team weren't optimists. On the other hand, they were willing to tackle this problem even though they thought the odds of succeeding were no better than world peace breaking out. In their own way, they were as delusional as my over-optimism sometimes made me.

As bizarre as it was, we were made for each other.

I leaned forward, a smile tugging at the corner of my mouth.

"I think I have an idea," I said.

I love writing this series and hope you have enjoyed this book. If you did, please consider leaving a review on Amazon. Even if it's only a few sentences, it would be a huge help. Thanks!

Beth Ann Blackwood
www.bablackwood.com

Made in the USA
Middletown, DE
17 January 2019